Foes before them, flames behind them,
ever east and onward eager rode they,
and folk fled them as the face of God,
till earth was empty, and no eyes saw them,
and no ears heard them in the endless hills,
save bird and beast baleful haunting
the lonely lands.   Thus at last came they
to Mirkwood's margin under mountain-shadows:
waste was behind them, walls before them;
on the houseless hills ever higher mounting   70
vast, unvanquished, lay the veiled forest.
Dark and dreary were the deep valleys,
where limbs gigantic of lowering trees
in endless aisles were arched o'er rivers
flowing down afar from fells of ice.
Among ruinous rocks ravens croaking
eagles answered in the air wheeling;
wolves were howling on the wood's border.
Cold blew the wind, keen and wintry,
in rising wrath from the rolling forest   80
among roaring leaves.   Rain came darkly,
and the sun was swallowed in sudden tempest.

The endless East in anger woke,
and black thunder born in dungeons
under mountains of menace moved above them.
There halted doubtful far high saw they
wan horsemen wild in windy clouds
grey and monstrous grimly riding
shadows-helmed to war, shapes disastrous.
Fierce grew the blast. Their fair banners   90
from their staves were stripped. Steel no longer,
gold nor silver nor gleaming shield
light reflected lost in darkness,
while phantom foes with fell voices

Lines 61–94 from Canto I of the latest version of the text
of *The Fall of Arthur*

THE FALL OF ARTHUR

Works by J.R.R. Tolkien

THE HOBBIT
LEAF BY NIGGLE
ON FAIRY-STORIES
FARMER GILES OF HAM
THE HOMECOMING OF BEORHTNOTH
THE LORD OF THE RINGS
THE ADVENTURES OF TOM BOMBADIL
THE ROAD GOES EVER ON (WITH DONALD SWANN)
SMITH OF WOOTTON MAJOR

Works published posthumously

SIR GAWAIN AND THE GREEN KNIGHT, PEARL AND SIR ORFEO
THE FATHER CHRISTMAS LETTERS
THE SILMARILLION
PICTURES BY J.R.R. TOLKIEN
UNFINISHED TALES
THE LETTERS OF J.R.R. TOLKIEN
FINN AND HENGEST
MR BLISS
THE MONSTERS AND THE CRITICS & OTHER ESSAYS
ROVERANDOM
THE CHILDREN OF HÚRIN
THE LEGEND OF SIGURD AND GUDRÚN

The History of Middle-earth – by Christopher Tolkien

I THE BOOK OF LOST TALES, PART ONE
II THE BOOK OF LOST TALES, PART TWO
III THE LAYS OF BELERIAND
IV THE SHAPING OF MIDDLE-EARTH
V THE LOST ROAD AND OTHER WRITINGS
VI THE RETURN OF THE SHADOW
VII THE TREASON OF ISENGARD
VIII THE WAR OF THE RING
IX SAURON DEFEATED
X MORGOTH'S RING
XI THE WAR OF THE JEWELS
XII THE PEOPLES OF MIDDLE-EARTH

THE FALL
OF ARTHUR

BY

J.R.R. Tolkien

Edited by Christopher Tolkien

HarperCollins*Publishers*

HarperCollins*Publishers*
77–85 Fulham Palace Road,
Hammersmith, London W6 8JB

www.tolkien.co.uk

www.tolkienestate.com

Published by HarperCollins*Publishers* 2013

1

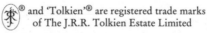

CONTENTS

FOREWORD

FOREWORD

It is well known that a prominent strain in my father's poetry
was his abiding love for the old 'Northern' alliterative verse,
which extended from the world of Middle-earth (notably in the
long but unfinished *Lay of the Children of Húrin*) to the dramatic dialogue *The Homecoming of Beorhtnoth* (arising from
the Old English poem *The Battle of Maldon*) and to his 'Old
Norse' poems *The New Lay of the Völsungs* and *The New Lay
of Gudrún* (to which he referred in a letter of 1967 as 'a thing
I did many years ago when trying to learn the art of writing
alliterative poetry'). In *Sir Gawain and the Green Knight* he
displayed his skill in his rendering of the alliterative verse of the
fourteenth century into the same metre in modern English. To
these is now added his unfinished and unpublished poem *The
Fall of Arthur*.

I have been able to discover no more than a single reference of any kind by my father to this poem, and that is in
a letter of 1955, in which he said: 'I write alliterative verse
with pleasure, though I have published little beyond the fragments in *The Lord of the Rings*, except 'The Homecoming
of Beorhtnoth' ... I still hope to finish a long poem on *The*

Fall of Arthur in the same measure' (*The Letters of J.R.R. Tolkien*, no.165). Nowhere among his papers is there any indication of when it was begun or when it was abandoned; but fortunately he preserved a letter written to him by R.W. Chambers on 9 December 1934. Chambers (Professor of English at University College, London), eighteen years his senior, was an old friend and strong supporter of my father, and in that letter he described how he had read *Arthur* on a train journey to Cambridge, and on the way back 'took advantage of an empty compartment to declaim him as he deserves'. He praised the poem with high praise: 'It is very great indeed ... really heroic, quite apart from its value in showing how the *Beowulf* metre can be used in modern English.' And he ended the letter 'You simply *must* finish it.'

But that my father did not do; and yet another of his long narrative poems was abandoned. It seems all but certain that he had ceased to work on the *Lay of the Children of Húrin* before he left the University of Leeds for Oxford in 1925, and he recorded that he began the *Lay of Leithian* (the legend of Beren and Lúthien), not in alliterative verse but in rhyming couplets, in the summer of that year (*The Lays of Beleriand*, p.3). In addition, while at Leeds he began an alliterative poem on *The Flight of the Noldoli from Valinor*, and another even briefer that was clearly the beginning of a *Lay of Eärendel* (*The Lays of Beleriand*, §II, *Poems Early Abandoned*).

I have suggested in *The Legend of Sigurd and Gudrún* (p.5) 'as a mere guess, since there is no evidence whatsoever to confirm it, that my father turned to the Norse poems as a new poetic enterprise [and a return to alliterative verse] after he abandoned the Lay of Leithian near the end of 1931.' If this were so, he must have begun work on *The Fall of Arthur*, which was still far from completion at the end of 1934, when the Norse poems had been brought to a conclusion.

In seeking some explanation of his abandonment of these ambitious poems when each was already far advanced, one might look to the circumstances of his life after his election to the Professorship of Anglo-Saxon at Oxford in 1925: the demands of his position and his scholarship and the needs and concerns and expenses of his family. As through so much of his life, he never had enough time; and it may be, as I incline to believe, that the breath of inspiration, endlessly impeded, could wither away; yet it would emerge again, when an opening appeared amid his duties and obligations – and his other interests, but now with a changed narrative impulse.

No doubt there were in fact specific reasons in each case, not now to be with any certainty discerned; but in that of *The Fall of Arthur* I have suggested (pp.149–55) that it was driven into the shallows by the great sea-changes that were taking place in my father's conceptions at that time, arising from his work on *The Lost Road* and the publication of *The Hobbit*: the emergence of Númenor, the myth of the World Made Round and the Straight Path, and the approach of *The Lord of the Rings*.

One might surmise also that the very nature of this last, elaborate poem made it peculiarly vulnerable to interruption or disturbance. The astonishing amount of surviving draft material for *The Fall of Arthur* reveals the difficulties inherent in such use of the metrical form that my father found so profoundly congenial, and his exacting and perfectionist concern to find, in an intricate and subtle narrative, fitting expression within the patterns of rhythm and alliteration of the Old English verse-form. To change the metaphor, *The Fall of Arthur* was a work of art to be built slowly: it could not withstand the rising of new imaginative horizons.

Whatever may be thought of these speculations, *The Fall of Arthur* necessarily entailed problems of presentation to the editor. It may be that some who take up this book would have been content with no more than the text of the poem as printed here, and perhaps a brief statement of the stages of its development, as attested by the abundant draft manuscripts. On the other hand, there may well be many others who, drawn to the poem by the attraction of its author but with little knowledge of 'the Arthurian legend', would wish, and expect, to find some indications of how this 'version' stands in relation to the mediaeval tradition from which it arose.

As I have said, my father left no indication even of the briefest kind, as he did of the 'Norse' poems published as *The Legend of Sigurd and Gudrún*, of his thought or intention that lay behind his very original treatment of 'The Legend of Lancelot and Guinevere'. But in the present case there is clearly no reason to enter the labyrinth in an editorial attempt to write a wide-ranging account of 'Arthurian' legend, which would very likely appear a forbidding rampart raised up as if it were a necessary preliminary to the reading of *The Fall of Arthur*.

I have therefore dispensed with any 'Introduction' properly so-called, but following the text of the poem I have contributed several commentaries, of a decidedly optional nature. The brief notes that follow the poem are largely confined to very concise explanations of names and words, and to references to the commentaries.

Each of these, for those who want such explorations, is concerned with a fairly distinct aspect of *The Fall of Arthur* and its special interest. The first of these, 'The Poem in Arthurian Tradition', simple in intent, avoiding speculative interpretation, and very limited in range, if somewhat lengthy, is an account of the derivation of my father's poem from particular narrative traditions and its divergences from them. For this purpose I have chiefly drawn upon two works in English, the mediaeval poem known as 'The Alliterative Morte Arthure', and the relevant tales of Sir Thomas Malory, with some reference to his sources. Not wishing to provide a mere dry précis, I have cited verbatim a number of passages from these works, as exemplifying those traditions in manner and mode that differ profoundly from this 'Alliterative Fall of Arthur' of another day.

After much deliberation I have thought it best, because much less confusing, to write this account as if the latest form of the poem (as printed in this book) were all that we could know of it, and the strange evolution of that form revealed by the analysis of the draft texts had therefore been lost. I have seen no need to enter into the shadowy origins of the Arthurian legend and the early centuries of its history, and I will only say here that it is essential to the understanding of *The Fall of Arthur* to recognize that the roots of the legend derive from the fifth century, after the final end of the Roman rule in Britain with the withdrawal of the legions in 410, and from memories of battles fought by Britons in resistance to the ruinous raids and encroachments of the barbarian invaders, Angles and Saxons, spreading from the eastern regions of their land. It is to be borne in mind that throughout this book the names *Britons* and *British* refer specifically and exclusively to the Celtic inhabitants and their language.

Following 'The Poem in Arthurian Tradition' is a discussion of 'The Unwritten Poem and its Relation to *The Silmarillion*', an account of the various writings that give some indication of my father's thoughts for the continuation of the poem; and then an account of 'The Evolution of the Poem', primarily an attempt to show as clearly as I could, granting the extremely complex textual history, the major changes of structure that I have referred to, together with much exemplification of his mode of composition.

Note. Throughout this book references to the text of the poem are given in the form canto number (Roman numeral) + line number, e.g. II.7.

THE FALL OF ARTHUR

I

How Arthur and Gawain went to war and rode into the East.

Arthur eastward   in arms purposed
his war to wage   on the wild marches,
over seas sailing   to Saxon lands,
from the Roman realm   ruin defending.
Thus the tides of time   to turn backward   5
and the heathen to humble,   his hope urged him,
that with harrying ships   they should hunt no more
on the shining shores   and shallow waters
of South Britain,   booty seeking.
As when the earth dwindles   in autumn days   10
and soon to its setting   the sun is waning
under mournful mist,   then a man will lust
for work and wandering,   while yet warm floweth
blood sun-kindled,   so burned his soul
after long glory   for a last assay   15
of pride and prowess,   to the proof setting
will unyielding   in war with fate.

I

So fate fell-woven   forward drave him,
and with malice Mordred   his mind hardened,
saying that war was wisdom   and waiting folly.   20
'Let their fanes be felled   and their fast places
bare and broken,   burned their havens,
and isles immune   from march of arms
or Roman reign   now reek to heaven
in fires of vengeance!   Fell thy hand is,   25
fortune follows thee – fare and conquer!
And Britain the blessed,   thy broad kingdom,
I will hold unharmed   till thy home-coming.
Faithful hast thou found me.   But what foe dareth
war here to wake   or the walls assail   30
of this island-realm   while Arthur liveth,
if the Eastern wolf   in his own forest
at last embayed   must for life battle?'
So Mordred spake,   and men praised him,
Gawain guessed not   guile or treason   35
in this bold counsel;   he was for battle eager,
in idle ease   the evil seeing
that had rent asunder   the Round Table.

Thus Arthur in arms   eastward journeyed,
and war awoke   in the wild regions.   40
Halls and temples   of the heathen kings
his might assailed   marching in conquest
from the mouths of the Rhine   o'er many kingdoms.

Lancelot he missed;   Lionel and Ector,
Bors and Blamore   to battle came not;   45
yet mighty lords   remained by him:
Bediver and Baldwin,   Brian of Ireland,
Marrac and Meneduc   from their mountain-towers;
Errac, and Iwain   of Urien's line
that was king in Reged;   Cedivor the strong   50
and the queen's kinsman   Cador the hasty.
Greatest was Gawain,   whose glory waxed
as times darkened,   true and dauntless,
among knights peerless   ever anew proven,
defence and fortress   of a falling world.   55
As in last sortie   from leaguered city
so Gawain led them.   As a glad trumpet
his voice was ringing   in the van of Arthur;
as a burning brand   his blade wielded
before the foremost   flashed as lightning.   60

Foes before them,   flames behind them,
ever east and onward   eager rode they,
and folk fled them   as the face of God,
till earth was empty,   and no eyes saw them,
and no ears heard them   in the endless hills,   65
save bird and beast   baleful haunting
the lonely lands.   Thus at last came they
to Mirkwood's margin   under mountain-shadows:
waste was behind them,   walls before them;

I

on the houseless hills   ever higher mounting   70
vast, unvanquished,   lay the veiled forest.
Dark and dreary   were the deep valleys,
where limbs gigantic   of lowering trees
in endless aisles   were arched o'er rivers
flowing down afar   from fells of ice.   75
Among ruinous rocks   ravens croaking
eagles answered   in the air wheeling;
wolves were howling   on the wood's border.
Cold blew the wind,   keen and wintry,
in rising wrath   from the rolling forest   80
among roaring leaves.   Rain came darkly,
and the sun was swallowed   in sudden tempest.

The endless East   in anger woke,
and black thunder   born in dungeons
under mountains of menace   moved above them.   85
Halting doubtful   there on high saw they
wan horsemen wild   in windy clouds
grey and monstrous   grimly riding
shadow-helmed to war,   shapes disastrous.
Fierce grew the blast.   Their fair banners   90
from their staves were stripped.   Steel no longer,
gold nor silver   nor gleaming shield
light reflected   lost in darkness,
while phantom foes   with fell voices
in the gloom gathered.   Gawain loudly   95

cried as a clarion.   Clear went his voice
in the rocks ringing   above roaring wind
and rolling thunder: 'Ride, forth to war,
ye hosts of ruin,   hate proclaiming!
Foes we fear not,   nor fell shadows   100
of the dark mountains   demon-haunted!
Hear now ye hills   and hoar forest,
ye awful thrones   of olden gods
huge and hopeless,   hear and tremble!
From the West comes war   that no wind daunteth,   105
might and purpose   that no mist stayeth;
lord of legions,   light in darkness,
east rides Arthur!'   Echoes were wakened.
The wind was stilled.   The walls of rock
'Arthur' answered.

               There evening came   110
with misty moon   moving slowly
through the wind-wreckage   in the wide heavens,
where strands of storm   among the stars wandered.
Fires were flickering,   frail tongues of gold
under hoary hills.   In the huge twilight   115
gleamed ghostly-pale,   on the ground rising
like elvish growths   in autumn grass
in some hollow of the hills   hid from mortals,
the tents of Arthur.

               Time wore onward.
Day came darkly,   dusky twilight   120

I

over gloomy heights   glimmering sunless;
in the weeping air   the wind perished.
Dead silence fell.   Out of deep valleys
fogs unfurling   floated upward;
dim vapours drowned,   dank and formless,   125
the hills under heaven,   the hollow places
in a fathomless sea   foundered sunken.
Trees looming forth   with twisted arms,
like weeds under water   where no wave moveth,
out of mist menaced   man forwandered.   130
Cold touched the hearts   of the host encamped
on Mirkwood's margin   at the mountain-roots.
They felt the forest   though the fogs veiled it;
their fires fainted.   Fear clutched their souls,
waiting watchful   in a world of shadow   135
for woe they knew not,   no word speaking.

Far and faintly   ere the fall of eve
they heard a horn   in the hills trembling,
forlorn and lonely,   like lost voices
out of night at sea.   Nearer it sounded.   140
Now hoofs they heard,   a horse neighing,
watchmen calling.   Woe had found them.
From the West came word,   winged and urgent,
of war assailing   the walls of Britain.
Lo! Cradoc was come   the king seeking   145

down perilous ways   their path trailing
from the mouths of the Rhine   o'er many kingdoms
grimly riding.   Neither grey shadows
nor mist stayed him   mighty-hearted.
Haggard and hungry   by his horse standing   150
to Arthur told he   evil tidings:
'Too long my lord   from your land ye tarry!
While war ye wage   on the wild peoples
in the homeless East,   a hundred chiefs
their seahorses   swift and deadly   155
have harnessed in havens   of the hidden islands.
Dragon-prowed they drive   over dark billows;
on shores unguarded   shields are gleaming
and black banners   borne amid trumpets.
Wild blow the winds   of war in Britain!   160
York is leaguered,   yielded Lincoln;
unto Kent kindled   the coast blazeth.
Hither have I hardly   hunted riding
on the sea pursued   to your side hastened,
treason to tell you.   Trust not Mordred!   165
He is false to faith,   your foes harbours,
with lords of Lochlan   league he maketh,
out of Almain and Angel   allies hireth,
coveting the kingdom,   to the crown reaching
hands unholy.   Haste now westward!'   170

*

I

A while then Arthur   white with anger
there sat in silence.   Thus sudden fortune
had turned and betrayed him.   In twenty battles
he had fought and conquered;   his foes were scattered,
neath his hand were humbled   heathen chieftains.   175
Now from hope's summit   headlong falling
his heart foreboded   that his house was doomed,
the ancient world   to its end falling,
and the tides of time   turned against him.

Swift then sent he   to summon Gawain   180
bold in counsel.   Bitter words he spake;
the evil tidings   all he told him.
'Now for Lancelot   I long sorely,
and we miss now most   the mighty swords
of Ban's kindred.   Best meseemeth   185
swift word to send,   service craving
to their lord of old.   To this leagued treason
we must power oppose,   proud returning
with matchless might   Mordred to humble.'

Gawain answered   grave and slowly: 190
'Best meseemeth   that Ban's kindred
abide in Benwick   and this black treason
favour nor further – yet I fear the worse:
thou wilt find thy friends   as foes meet thee.

24

If Lancelot   hath loyal purpose   195
let him prove repentance,   his pride forgoing,
uncalled coming   when his king needeth!
But fainer with fewer   faithfulhearted
would I dare danger,   than with doubtful swords
and tarnished shields   of truant lieges   200
our muster swell.   Why more need we?
Though thou legions levy   through the lands of Earth,
fay or mortal,   from the Forest's margin
to the Isle of Avalon,   armies countless,
never and nowhere   knights more puissant,   205
nobler chivalry   of renown fairer,
mightier manhood   under moon or sun
shall be gathered again   till graves open.
Here free unfaded   is the flower of time
that men shall remember   through the mist of years   210
as a golden summer   in the grey winter.
And Gawain hast thou.   May God keep us
in hope allied,   heart united,
as the kindred blood   in our bodies courseth,
Arthur and Gawain!   Evil greater   215
hath fled aforetime   that we faced together.
Now in haste is hope!   While hate lingers,
and uncertain counsel   secret ponders,
as wroth as wind   let us ride westward,
and sail over sea   with sudden vengeance!'   220

*

II

How the Frisian ship brought news, and Mordred gathered his
    host and went to Camelot seeking the queen.

Dark wind came driving   over deep water,
from the South sweeping   surf upon the beaches,
a roaring sea   rolling endless
huge hoarcrested   hills of thunder.
The world darkened.   Wan rode the moon   5
through stormy clouds   streaming northward.

From France came flying   a fleet vessel
dark and dragon-prowed,   dreadly carven,
sable-shrouded,   on the sea leaping,
by the waves hunted   as a wild creature   10
among hungry hounds.   The horns of the wind
were its mort blowing.   Men were calling,
to their gods crying   with grim voices,
as it rode to wreck   with riven timbers
in the mouths of the sea.   The moon glittered   15

in the glaring eyes   upon their grey faces
death outstaring.   Doom o'ercame them.

Mordred was waking.   His mind wandered
in dark counsels   deep and secret.
From a window looked he   in western tower: 20
drear and doubtful   day was breaking,
grey light glimmered   behind gates of cloud.
About the walls of stone   wind was flowing;
sea sighed below,   surging, grinding.
He heard nor heeded: his heart returned   25
to its long thraldom   lust-tormented,
to Guinever the golden   with gleaming limbs,
as fair and fell   as fay-woman
in the world walking   for the woe of men
no tear shedding.   Towers might he conquer,   30
and thrones o'erthrow   yet the thought quench not.

In her blissful bower   on bed of silver
softly slept she   on silken pillows
with long hair loosened,   lightly breathing,
in fragrant dreams   fearless wandering,   35
of pity and repentance   no pain feeling,
in the courts of Camelot   queen and peerless,
queen unguarded.   Cold blew the wind.
His bed was barren;   there black phantoms

II

of desire unsated   and savage fury   40
in his brain had brooded   till bleak morning.

A stair he mounted   steeply winding
to walls embattled   well-wrought of stone.
O'er the weeping world   waking coldly
he leant and laughed,   lean and tearless.   45
Cocks were crowing.   Clamour rose at gate.
Servants sought him   soft-foot running
through hall and bower   hunting swiftly.
His eager squire   Ivor hailed him
by the dungeon-stair   at the door standing: 50
'Lord! Come below!   Why alone walk ye?
Tidings await you!   Time is spared us
too short for shrift.   A ship is landed!'

Mordred came then;   and men trembled
at his dark visage   drenched with water;   55
wind-tossed his hair,   and his words grated:
'Do ye ransack with rabble   this royal castle,
Because a ship from storm   to shore flieth?'
Ivor him answered: 'On your errand hasting
the Frisian captain   from France cometh   60
on wings of wind,   his word keeping,
fate defying.   Fate hath conquered.
His ship is broken   on the shore lying;
at the door of death   he doomed lingers.

All else are dead.'   At early day   65
the red rover   the rings of gold
repayed to his patron,   ere he passed to hell;
shrift he sought not,   nor shaven priest,
his latest words   to his lord speaking:
'Cradoc the accurséd   to the king flying   70
through thy net slipping   news untimely
east to Almain   ere the hour was ripe
hath brought from Britain.   Bare is thy counsel;
in Arthur's ears   all is rumoured
of thy deeds and purpose.   Dark his anger.   75
He hastens home, and his   host summons,
from the Roman marches   riding as tempest.
Nine thousand knights   draw near the sea;
on northern waves   his navy lies,
Whitesand with boats,   wherries and barges   80
shipwrights' hammers,   shouting seamen,
ringing armour,   riders hasting,
is loud and thronging.   Look ye to it!
Shining on bulwarks   shields are hanging
blazoned in blood-red   foreboding war.   85
On the waves they wait   and the wind's fury;
lean hounds at leash   longships are tugging
on heaving hawsers.   Haste now eastward!'

Radbod the Red,   rover fearless,
heathen-hearted   to hate faithful,   90

II

died as his doom was.   Dark was the morning.
To sea they cast him,   of his soul recked not
that walks in the waters,   wandering homeless.

Wild rode the wind   through the West country.
Banners were blowing,   black was the raven   95
they bore as blazon.   Blaring of trumpets,
neighing of horses,   gnashing of armour,
in the hoar hollows   of the hills echoed.
Mordred was marching;   messengers speeding
northward and eastward   the news bearing   100
through the land of Logres.   Lords and chieftains
to his side he summoned   swift to hasten
their tryst keeping,   true to Mordred,
faithful in falsehood,   foes of Arthur,
lovers of treason,   lightly purchased   105
followers of fortune,   and freebooters
of Erin and Alban   and East-Sassoin,
of Almain and Angel   and the isles of mist;
the crows of the coast   and the cold marshes.

He came to Camelot,   the queen seeking.   110
Fiercely heard she   his feet hasten
with striding steps   the stair climbing.
To her bower came he.   With burning eyes
by the door he stood   darkly gazing.

She sat silent   no sign giving   115
at the wide window.   Wan gleamed the day
in her bright tresses   bleakly golden.
Grey her eyes were   as a glittering sea;
glass-clear and chill   they his glance challenged
proud and pitiless.   But pale her cheek   120
for heart misgave her,   as one that hounds tameth
to follow her feet   and fawn at hand,
when wolf unawares   walks among them.

Then spake Mordred   with his mouth smiling:
'Hail! Lady of Britain!   It is long sitting   125
alone lordless   in loveless days,
a kingless queen   in courts that echo
to no noise of knighthood.   Yet never shalt thou
on earth hereafter   thine hours barren
and life find loveless.   Nor less than queen   130
with dimmed glory   thy days revile
though chances change – if thou choose aright.
A king courts thee   his crown to share,
his love offering   and loyal service.'

Gravely Guinever   again answered: 135
'Thou callest thee king,   and of crown speakest –
in his lieu 'twas lent thee   by thy liege-master,
who liveth yet and reigneth,   though long absent.

II

For thy love I thank thee   and loyal service,
though due I deem it   from dear nephew   140
to Arthur's queen.'   Then her eyes wavered,
and he set her beside him,   seized her fiercely.
Grim words he spake – Guinever trembled:
'Now never again   from northern wars
shall Arthur enter   this island realm,   145
nor Lancelot du Lake   love remembering
to thy tryst return!   Time is changing;
the West waning,   a wind rising
in the waxing East.   The world falters.
New tides are running   in the narrrow waters.   150
False or faithful,   only fearless man
shall ride the rapids   from ruin snatching
power and glory.   I purpose so.
Thou at my side shall lie,   slave or lady,
as thou wilt or wilt not,   wife or captive.   155
This treasure take I,   ere towers crumble,
and thrones are o'erturned,   thirst first will I slake.
I will be king after   and crowned with gold.'

Then the queen took counsel   in her cold bosom
between fear and prudence;   feigning wonder,   160
softly after silence   she dissembling spake:
'My lord, unlooked-for   were thy love-speeches,
and this eager suit   thou urgest now;

new thoughts arise   needing counsel!
Delay allow me   and a little respite   165
ere thou ask my answer!   Should Arthur come,
my plight were perilous.   Could thou proof show me
that thou wilt ride over ruin,   wresting kingship
from troublous times,   troth were plighted
with briefer counsel.'   Bitterly laughed he: 170
'What proof of power   shall prisoner seek,
captive of captor?   Be I king or earl,
'twixt bride and bond   brief be the choosing!
Needs must tonight   that I know thy mind;
longer I grant not.'   Then his leave took he.   175
Fierce and hasty   his feet echoed
with striding steps   on the stone pavement.

Night came slowly.   The naked moon
slipped sudden forth   from swathing clouds
torn by tempest,   in a tarn of stars   180
swam serenely.   Riding swiftly
hosemen hastened.   Hooves were beating,
steel-pointed spears   stung with silver.
Long leagues behind   in a low valley
the lights of Camelot   lessened and faded;   185
before lay forest   and the far marches,
dark roads and dim.   Dread pursued them.
Wolf had wakened   in the woods stalking,

II

and the hind hardly   from hiding driven
her foe had fled,   fear-bewildered,   190
cowed and hunted,   once queen of herds
for whom harts majestic   in horned combat
had fought fiercely.   So fled she now,
Guinevere the fair   in grey mantled,
cloaked in darkness,   from the courts stealing.   195
Few faithful men   her flight aided,
folk that followed her   in former days,
when from Leodegrance   to Logres rode
bride to bridegroom   brave and golden
in mighty Arthur's   morning glory.   200
Now to lonely towers,   land deserted,
where Leodegrance   once long ago
at the Round Table   regal feasted,
she hastened home   to harbour cold,
hiding uncertain.   In her heart darkly   205
she thought of Lancelot,   should he learn afar
of her woe and wandering   by wolf hunted.
If the king were conquered,   and the crows feasted,
would he come at her call,   queen and lady
riding to rescue?   Then from ruin haply   210
were gladness wrested.   Guinevere the fair,
not Mordred only,   should master chance
and the tides of time   turn to her purpose.

*

III

_____

Of Sir Lancelot, who abode in Benwick.

In the South from sleep   to swift fury
a storm was stirred,   striding northward
over leagues of water   loud with thunder
and roaring rain   it rushed onward.
Their hoary heads   hills and mountains   5
tossed in tumult   on the towering seas.
On Benwick's beaches   breakers pounding
ground gigantic   grumbling boulders
with ogre anger.   The air was salt
with spume and spindrift   splashed to vapour.   10

There Lancelot   over leagues of sea
in heaving welter   from a high window
looked and wondered   alone musing.
Dark slowly fell.   Deep his anguish.
He his lord betrayed   to love yielding,   15
and love forsaking   lord regained not;

III

faith was refused him   who had faith broken,
by leagues of sea   from love sundered.

Sir Lancelot,   Lord of Benwick
of old was the noblest   knight of Arthur,   20
among sons of kings   kingly seeming,
deemed most daring,   in deeds of arms
all surpassing,   eagerhearted;
among folk whose beauty   as a flower blossomed
in face the fairest,   formed in manhood   25
strong and gracious,   steel well-tempered.
White his hue was;   his hair raven,
dark and splendid;   dark his eyes were.
Gold was Gawain,   gold as sunlight,
but grey his eyes were   gleaming keenly;   30
his mood sterner.   By men holden
almost equal   envy he knew not,
peer and peerless   praising justly,
but to his lord alone   his love giving;
no man nor woman   in his mind holding   35
dearer than Arthur.   Daily watchful
the Queen he doubted,   ere the cold shadow
on her great glory   grey had fallen.

To Lancelot   her love gave she,
in his great glory   gladness finding.   40

To his lady only   was his love given;
no man nor woman   in his mind held he
than Guinever dearer: glory only,
knighthood's honour,   near his lady
in his heart holding.   High his purpose;   45
he long was loyal   to his lord Arthur,
among the Round Table's   royal order
prince and peerless,   proudly serving
Queen and lady.   But cold silver
or glowing gold   greedy-hearted   50
in her fingers taken   fairer thought she,
more lovely deeming   what she alone treasured
darkly hoarded.   Dear she loved him
with love unyielding,   lady ruthless,
fair as fay-woman   and fell-minded   55
in the world walking   for the woe of men.
Fate sent her forth.   Fair she deemed him
beyond gold and silver   to her grasp lying.
Silver and golden,   as the sun at morning
her smile dazzled,   and her sudden weeping   60
with tears softened,   tender poison,
steel well-tempered.   Strong oaths they broke.

Mordred in secret   mirthless watched them
betwixt hate and envy,   hope and torment.
Thus was bred the evil,   and the black shadow   65

III

o'er the courts of Arthur   as a cloud growing
dimmed the daylight   darkling slowly.
In evil hour   was Agravain
the dour-handed   to death smitten –
by the door fell he – dear to Gawain.   70
Swift swords were drawn   by sworn brethren
and the Round Table   rent asunder
in the Queen's quarrel.   Cold rang the blades.
The Queen was taken.   With cruel justice
fair as fay-woman   they to fire doomed her,   75
to death they condemned her.   But death waited.
There Lancelot   as lightning came
amid riding thunder   ruthless flaming
in sudden assault   sweeping heedless
he friends of old   felled and trampled,   80
as trees by tempest   torn uprooted.
Gaheris and Gareth   Gawain's brethren
by the fire fell they   as fate willed it.
From the fire he snatched her;   far he bore her;
fear fell on men,   none would follow after;   85
for Ban's kindred   in their battle closed him.

Then rage left him,   and his wrath sickened,
his mood faltered.   He mourned too late
in ruth for the rending   of the Round Table.
His pride he repented,   his prowess cursing   90

that friends had felled,   faith had broken.
For the love longing   of his lord Arthur
he would heal yet honour   with his heart's anguish,
and the queen restore,   by the king's mercy
her estate restablish.   Strange she deemed him   95
by a sudden sickness   from his self altered.
From war she shrank not,   might her will conquer,
life both and love   with delight keeping
to wield as she wished   while the world lasted;
but little liked her   lonely exile,   100
or for love to lose   her life's splendour.
In sorrow they parted.   With searing words
his wound she probed   his will searching.
Grief bewrayed her   and greed thwarted;
the shining sun   was sudden shaded   105
in storm of darkness.   Strange he deemed her
from her self altered.   By the sea stood he
as a graven stone   grey and hopeless.
In pain they parted.   Pardon found she
by her king's mercy,   and men's counsel,   110
lest worse befall,   war unholy
among Christian kings,   while the crows feasted.
In the courts of Camelot   she was queen again
great and glorious.   Grace with Arthur
he sought and found not.   They his sword refused.   115
On that knee no more,   knight in fealty

III

might he hilt handle,   nor his head there lay,
not Lancelot,   love forsaking,
pardon asking,   with pride humbled.
Loveforsaken,   from the land banished,   120
from the Round Table's   royal order
and his siege glorious   where he sat aforetime
he went sadly.   The salt water
lay grey behind him.
       Grief knew Arthur
in his heart's secret,   and his house him seemed   125
in mirth minished,   marred in gladness,
his noblest knight   in his need losing.
Not alone to his land   over loud waters
went Lancelot.   Lords of his kindred
were many and mighty.   At their masts floated   130
the banners of Blamore   and of Bors the strong,
of Lionel, Lavain,   and loyal Ector,
Ban's younger son.   They to Benwick sailed
Britain forsaking.   In battle no more
to Arthur's aid   their arms bore they,   135
but in the towers of Ban   tall and dauntless
watchful dwelt they,   war refusing,
Lancelot their lord   with love guarding
in his days of darkness.   Deep his anguish.
He lord betrayed   to love yielding,   140

and love forsaking   lord regained not,
by leagues of sea   from love sundered.

From western havens   word was rumoured
of Arthur arming   against his own kingdom,
how a mighty navy   manned with vengeance   145
he swift assembled   that the sudden fury
of striding storm   stayed and hindered.
Of the Lord of Logres,   and the leagued treason
that his throne threatened,   thought he darkly:
now they need would know   of knights faithful   150
to uphold on high   the holy crown,
the west still to wield   by the waves' margin,
walls defending   against the world's ruin;
now they most would miss   the mighty swords
of Ban's kindred   and their banners gleaming;   155
now Lancelot   his lord's battle
should fill with fire   as a flame shining.

Then half he hoped,   and half wished not,
to receive summons,   swift commandment,
to king the allegiance   loyal recalling   160
of Lancelot   to his lord Arthur.
Of Guinever again   grieving thought he:
there was woe in Britain,   war was kindled;
were her faith renewed   firm and steadfast,

41

III

then she stood in danger.   Dear he loved her.   165
Though in wrath she left him,   no ruth showing,
no pity feeling,   proud and scornful,
dear he loved her.   When danger threatened,
if she sent him summons,   swift and gladly
against tide and tempest   trumpet sounding,   170
he would sail overseas,   sword unsheathing
in land forlorn   at the last battle
by his lady bidden,   though his lord shunned him.

But there came neither   from king summons
nor word from lady.   Only wind journeyed   175
over wide waters   wild and heedless.
Now Gawain's glory,   golden riding
as the westering sun   that the world kindles
ere he red sinketh   by the rim of ocean,
before Arthur blazed,   while the East darkened.   180
Guinever hiding   in the grey shadow
watched and waited,   while the world faltered;
grimhearted grown   as gladness waned
danger weighed she   in her dark counsel,
her hope in havoc,   in her heart thinking   185
men's fate to mould   to her mind's purpose.
And Lancelot   over leagues of sea
looked and pondered   alone musing
doubtful-hearted.   Dark had fallen.

No horn he blew,   no host gathered;   190
he wavered and went not.   Wind was roaring
the towers trembled   tempest-shaken.

Dawn came dimly.   On the dun beaches
the foam glimmered   faint and ghostly;
the tide was turning,   tempest waning.   195
Light leapt upward   from the long shadow,
and walking on the water   waves kindled,
as glass glittering   green and silver.
In sombre sleep   by the sill drooping
lay Lancelot   alone dreaming;   200
his head was bowed   by the high window.
His eyes opened   upon early day:
the wind still walked   in the wide heaven
lofty faring,   but on lowly earth
peace had fallen.   Pools reflected   205
the slanting sun   silver gleaming;
washed with water   the world shimmered;
bird sang to bird   blithe at morning.

His heart arose,   as were heavy burden
lightly lifted.   Alone standing   210
with the flame of morn   in his face burning
the surge he felt   of song forgotten
in his heart moving   as a harp-music.

III

There Lancelot,   low and softly
to himself singing,   the sun greeted,   215
life from darkness   lifted shining
in the dome of heaven   by death exalted.
Ever times would change   and tides alter,
and o'er hills of morning   hope come striding
to awake the weary,   while the world lasted.   220

The hour he knew not,   that never after
it would return in time,   tempest bringing,
to war calling   with the wind's trumpet.
The tides of chance   had turned backward,
their flood was passed   flowing swiftly.   225
Death was before him,   and his day setting
beyond the tides of time   to return never
among waking men,   while the world lasted.

*

IV

_____

How Arthur returned at morn and by Sir Gawain's hand won
the passage of the sea.

Wolves were howling on the wood's border;
the windy trees   wailed and trembled,
and wandering leaves   wild and homeless
drifted dying in the deep hollows.
Dark lay the road   through dank valleys   5
among mounting hills   mist-encircled
to the walls of Wales   in the west frowning
brownfaced and bare.   To the black mountains
horsemen hastened,   on the houseless stones
no track leaving.   Tumbling waters   10
from the fells falling,   foaming in darkness,
they heard as they passed   to the hidden kingdom.
Night fell behind.   The noise of hooves
was lost in silence   in a land of shadow.

*

IV

Dawn came dimly.   On the dark faces   15
of the old mountains   eastward staring
light was kindled.   The land shimmered.
Sun came shining.   Silver morning
bathed in water   bright ascended
the bare heaven   blue and lofty.   20
Beams fell slanting   through the boughs of trees
glancing and glimmering   in the grey forest;
rain drops running   from rustling leaves
like drops of glass   dripped and glistened.
No beast was stirring: the birds listened.   25
As wary as wolves   through the wood stalking
to the marches rode there   Mordred's hunters,
huge and hungry   hounds beside them
the fewte followed   fiercely baying.
The queen they hunted   with cold hatred   30
till their hope failed them   amid houseless stones,
halting hungry-eyed   under the hills' menace
at the walls of Wales.   War was behind them
and woe in Britain.   Winds were shifting,
Mordred waiting.
                    Their message found him   35
by the seaward cliffs   in the south-country
sheer and shining.   Upon shaven grass
his tents were marshalled,   as a town clustered
with lanes and alleys   loud with voices

in the dales hidden   and on downs rising   40
above Romeril   where running water
to the shore had cloven   a shallow pathway.
From the East, from Angel   and the isles of mist,
there kings of Almain   their craft mustered,
under cliff crowding   their carven prows   45
and black banners   in the breeze flying.
Fair wind came foaming   over flecked water,
on gleaming shingle   green and silver
the waves were washing   on walls of chalk.
On a mound of grass   Mordred stood there: 50
ever gazed his eyes   out and southward,
lest Arthur's ships   unawares to shore
the winds should waft.   Watchmen he posted
by the sea's margin   in the south-country,
by night and day   the narrow waters   55
from the hills to heed.   There on high raised he
builded beacons   that should blaze with fire,
if Arthur came,   to his aid calling
his men to muster   where he most needed.
Thus he watched and waited   and the wind studied. 60

Ivor hailed him   with eager voice
by his tent standing   tall and brooding;
words unwelcome   from the West brought he.
'O King!' he cried,   'the Queen is lost!

IV

Her trail faded   in the trackless stones;   65
hound and hunter   in the hills faltered.
To the hidden kingdom   and the holy vales
where Leodegrance   once long ago
lived beleaguered,   lord enchanted,
she hath fled and is free.   But few love her.   70
Fear her no longer,   the fay-woman!
Fell fate take her!   May her feet never
return hither   to trouble Mordred!
From thy mind thrust her!   With men deal thou,
woman forsaking   and to war turning!   75
Thine hour is at hand.'   Then his eyes wavered
and his tongue halted.   Turning slowly
with frown of thunder   fiercely Mordred
gazed on him glaring.   'Begone!' cried he.
'The master's hour   master chooseth.   80
Nought thou knowest.   At need failing
from vain errand   dost venture home
with tongue untamed   to teach Mordred
thy fool's counsel?   Flee mine anger
unto foul fortune.   The fiend take thee!'   85

Alone then long   lowering paced he.
In his bosom there burned   under black shadow
a smouldering fire   whose smoke choked him;
his mind wavered   in a maze walking

between fear and fury.   At first his thought   90
hunger-hunted   from his hold wandered
by lust allured   to its long torment.
But he guessed that Guinever   had greeting sent
by secret servant   over sea speeding
to Lancelot,   love recalling   95
and his aid asking   in her evil day.
Should Ban's kindred   to battle hasten
and the fair lily   on the field sable
once more be seen   marching proudly
Arthur to strengthen,   ill were boded   100
to his plot and purpose.   Thus he pondered long.
For Lancelot,   lord of Benwick,
most he hated   and yet most dreaded,
and words of witchcraft   well remembered
that lords of Benwick   the lily bearing   105
in open battle   should he ever challenge
he would reap ruin.   Thus wrath with cunning,
doubt with daring   in his dark counsel
warred uncertain.   The wind lessened.
In cloudless sky   clear and golden   110
the sun at evening   summer rekindled
in a glow sinking.   The sea glimmered
under streaming stars   in the steep heaven.
Day followed day.   Dawn came brightly
with a breeze blowing   blithe at morning   115

IV

cool and keenwingéd.   A cry woke him.
'A sail, a sail   on the sea shining!'
Watchmen were calling,   wailing voices
from ward to ward   the wind carried,
and grasping brands   guards by the beacons   120
wakeful waited.   No word gave he.
Eager went his eyes   out and southward,
and sails saw he   on the sea climbing.
Thus came Arthur   at early morn
at last returning   to his lost kingdom.   125
On his shrouds there shone   sheen with silver
a white lady   in holy arms
a babe bearing   born of maiden.
Sun shone through them.   The sea sparkled.
Men marked it well,   Mordred knew it,   130
Arthur's ensign.   Yet his eyes wandered;
for the banner of Benwick   breathless looked he,
silver upon sable.   But he saw it not.
The fair flower-de-luce   on its field withered
drooping in darkness.   Doom came nearer.   135
The sun mounted   and the sails whitened.
Far over the sea   faintly sounding
trumpets heard they.   Towering upward
from Arthur's side   eager hastened
a mighty ship   in the morn gleaming   140
high, white-timbered,   with hull gilded;
on its sail was sewn   a sun rising,

on its broidered banner   in the breeze floated
a fiery griffon   golden flaming.
Thus came Gawain   his king guarding   145
valiant-hearted   the vaward leading:
a hundred ships   with hulls shining
and shrouds swelling   and shields swinging.
Behind beheld they   the host faring:
deepweighed dromonds   and drawn barges,   150
galleys and galleons   with gear of war,
six hundred sail   in the sun turning,
fair sight and fell.   Flags were streaming;
ten thousand told   targes hung there
bright on the bulwarks,   blazons of princes   155
and knights of the North   and the nine kingdoms
of Britain the blessed.   But Ban's kindred,
and Lancelot   with his lilies came not.

Then Mordred laughed   loud and mirthless.
Word he shouted.   Wild were the trumpets.   160
Beacons were blazing,   banners were lifted,
shaft rang on shield,   and the shores echoed.
War was awakened   and woe in Britain.
Thus came Arthur   to his own kingdom
in power and majesty   proud returning   165
to Romeril   where running slowly
by the shore now weeps   a shuddering water.

IV

Sun shone on swords. Silver-pointed
the spears sparkled   as they sprang upward,
white as wheatfield. Wheeling above them   170
the crows were crying   with cold voices.
In the foaming sea   flashed a thousand
swift oars sweeping. Saxon chieftains
at their stems standing   sternly shouted;
blades they brandished   and broad axes,   175
on their gods calling   with grim voices.
With dread faces   dragon-prowed they spurred
their sea-horses   to sudden onset,
swerving swifly   and swinging inward.
Beak met bulwark. Burst were timbers.   180
There was clang of iron   and crash of axes;
sparked and splintered   spears and helmets;
the smiths of battle   on smitten anvils
there dinned and hammered   deadly forging
wrath and ruin. Red their hands were.   185
About Prydwen pressed they,   the proud and fair,
the ship of Arthur   with sheen of silver.

Then Gawain sounded   his glad trumpet.
His great galleon   golden shining
as thunder riding   thrust among them   190
with wind behind her. In her wake followed
lieges of Lothian,   lords and captains.

52

Oars were splintered.   Iron clave timber,
and ropes were riven.   With rending crash
masts dismantled   as mountain-trees   195
rushed down rattling   in the roar of battle.
Now grim Galuth   Gawain brandished
his sword renowned – smiths enchanted
ere Rome was built   with runes marked it
and its steel tempered   strong and deadly –   200
forth leapt he as fire   a flame wielding.
The king of Gothland   on his carven prow
he smote to death   and to sea drave him;
upon lords of Lochlan   lightning hurled he,
helms boar-crested,   heathen standards   205
hewed asunder.   High rang his voice
'Arthur' calling.   The air trembled
with thunderous answer   thousandfolded.
As straw from storm,   as stalks falling
before reapers ruthless,   as roke flying   210
before the rising sun   wrathful blazing
his foemen fled.   Fear o'ercame them.
From board and beam   beaten fell they,
in the sea they sank   their souls losing.
Boats were blazing,   burned and smoking;   215
some on shore shivered   to shards broken.
Red ran the tide   the rocks staining.
Shields on the water   shorn and splintered

IV

as flotsam floated.   Few saved their lives
broken and bleeding   from that battle flying.   220
Thus came Arthur   to his own kingdom
and the sea's passage   with the sword conquered,
Gawain leading.   Now his glory shone
as the star of noon   stern and cloudless
o'er the heads of men   to its height climbing   225
ere it fall and fail.   Fate yet waited.
Tide was turning.   Timbers broken,
dead men and drowned,   a dark jetsam,
were left to lie   on the long beaches;
rocks robed with red   rose from water.   230

*

V

Of the setting of the sun at Romeril.

Thus Arthur abode   on the ebb riding.
At his land he looked   and longed sorely
on the grass again   there green swaying,
to walk at his will,   while the world lasted;
the sweet to savour   of salt mingled   5
with wine-scented   waft of clover
over sunlit turf   seaward leaning,
in kindly Christendom   the clear ringing
of bells to hear   on the breeze swaying,
a king of peace   kingdom wielding   10
in a holy realm   beside Heaven's gateway.

On the land he looked   lofty shining.
Treason trod there   trumpets sounding
in power and pride.   Princes faithless
on shore their shields   shameless marshalled,   15
their king betraying,   Christ forsaking,

55

V

to heathen might   their hope turning.
Men were mustering   marching southward,
from the East hurried   evil horsemen
as plague of fire   pouring ruinous;   20
white towers were burned,   wheat was trampled,
the ground groaning   and the grass withered.
There was woe in Britain   and the world faded;
bells were silent,   blades were ringing
hell's gate was wide   and heaven distant.   25

Toll must he pay   and trewage grievous,
the blood spending   that he best treasured
the lives losing   that he loved dearest;
there friends should fall   and the flower wither
of fair knighthood,   for faith earning   30
the death and darkness,   doom of mortals,
ere the walls were won   or the way conquered,
or the grass again   there green springing
his feet should feel   faring homeward.
Never had Arthur   need or danger   35
tamed or daunted,   turned from purpose
or his path hindered.   Now pity whelmed him
and love of his land   and his loyal people,
for the low misled   and the long-tempted,
the weak that wavered,   for the wicked grieving.   40
With woe and weariness   and war sated,
kingship owning   crowned and righteous

56

he would pass in peace   pardon granting,
the hurt healing   and the whole guiding,
to Britain the blessed   bliss recalling.   45
Death lay between   dark before him
ere the way were won   or the world conquered.

[The next sixteen lines were written more hastily on a separate
slip of paper.]

For Gawain he called.   Gravely speaking
dark thoughts he showed   in his deep trouble.
'Liege and kinsman   loyal and noble,   50
my tower and targe,   my true counsel,
the path before us   to peril leadeth.
We have won the water.   The walls remain,
and manned with menace   might defy they.
Do we rightly choose   ruthless onset,   55
to traitor keeper   toll of death
to pay for passage,   no price counting,
on dread venture   at disadvantage
all hope to hazard?   My heart urgeth
that best it were   that battle waited.   60
To other landing   our arms leading
let us trust the wind   and tide ebbing
to waft us westward.'

Here ends *The Fall of Arthur* in its latest form.

NOTES ON THE TEXT OF
THE FALL OF ARTHUR

Canto I

1–9   On King Arthur's campaign into eastern regions see pp.86–8.

21   *fanes*: temples.

33   *at last embayed* (a pencilled correction of *embayed and leaguered*): No such meaning of a verb *embay* is recorded in the *Oxford English Dictionary*, but the sense is obviously 'brought to bay'.

44–50   Knights of the Round Table. Lionel and Ector (on whom see pp.193–7), Bors and Blamore, were kinsmen of Lancelot: Ector was his younger brother. Bedivere is only named here in *The Fall of Arthur*, but he would no doubt have played a part in the aftermath of the battle of Camlan, if my father had reached so far in his narrative (see pp.112–14).

        Marrac and Meneduc and Errac are named in the alliterative *Morte Arthure* among the slain at Camlan.

        Reged was the name of a forgotten kingdom in North Britain. Urien king of Reged and his son Iwain

(Ówein) seem to have been in origin historical kings, who became famous in the wars of the North Britons against the Angles in the sixth century.

Several of these knights appear in *Sir Gawain and the Green Knight*: Lionel, Bors, Bedivere, Errac, Iwain son of Urien (in my father's translation, stanzas 6 and 24).

51   *Cador the hasty*: my father wrote *fearless* but later pencilled in *hasty* above. One might suppose that in making this change he was thinking of the incident described by Geoffrey of Monmouth, when the letter from the Emperor Lucius was read (see p.77). Geoffrey called Cador, Duke of Cornwall, a 'merry' man (*erat laeti animi*): he burst out laughing on that occasion, urging that the Roman challenge be welcomed, for the Britons had become soft and slothful. In Laȝamon's *Brut* (p.78) Cador declared *For nauere ne lufede ich longe grið inne mine londe* ('for never loved I long peace in my land'), and for this he was roundly rebuked by Gawain. But in *The Fall of Arthur* (I.36–8) it was Gawain who

> was for battle eager,
> in idle ease   the evil seeing
> that had rent asunder   the Round Table.

130   *forwandered*: wearied with wandering.

145   *Cradoc*: see p.84.

160   *Wild blow the winds of war in Britain!*: see p.89.

167   *Lochlan*: the name of a land in Irish legend, here it
        seems suggesting a remote people hostile to Arthur;
        it is repeated in IV.204.

168   *Almain*: Germany; *Angel*: the ancient homeland of
        the Angles in the Danish peninsula.

185, 191–2 *Ban's kindred*: King Ban of Benwick in France
        was the father of Sir Lancelot; see p.102.

203–4   *From the Forest's margin / to the Isle of Avalon*: see
        p.145.

12   *mort*: the note blown on a horn at the death of a hunted deer.

27   *Guinever*: my father's spelling of the Queen's name was very various. *Guinever* preponderates, but in the latest text of Canto II, while *Guinever* appears at lines 27, 135, and 143, it is *Guinevere* at 194 and 211; and in the text preceding the last the spellings are *Guinevere, Gwenevere, Gwenever.*

50   *the dungeon-stair*: *dungeon* is here used in the old sense of the keep or great central tower of a medieval castle.

52–3   *Time is spared us / too short for shrift.* In the earliest version of the canto the text here reads *The sea spares us / a shrift too short* (p.215). The original meaning of 'short shrift' was a short space of time in which to make a confession (*shrift*) before death; hence, a brief respite. Cf. II.68 *shrift he sought not.*

80   *Whitesand*: Wissant in the Pas-de-Calais, between Calais and Boulogne.

86   *On the waves they wait and the wind's fury*: i.e. they wait until the waves and the wind abate.

101   *Logres*: the kingdom of Britain ruled by King Arthur.

107–8 *Erin*: Ireland; *Alban*: Scotland; *East-Sassoin*: East Saxony. For *Almain* and *Angel* see note to I.168.

198, 202–3 *Leodegrance*: King of Camiliard in Wales, father of Guinevere. The mention of the Round Table at line 203 is a reference to the legend that it was made for Uther Pendragon, Arthur's father. In Malory's *Tale of King Arthur* Leodegrance learned of Merlin that Arthur wished to have Guinevere for his wife:

'That is to me,' seyde kyng Leodegreauns, 'the beste tydynges that ever I herde, that so worthy a kyng of prouesse and noblesse wol wedde my doughter. And as for my londis, I wolde geff hit hym yf I wyste hyt myght please hym, but he hath londis inow, he nedith none. But I shall sende hym a gyffte that shal please hym muche more, for I shall gyff hym the Table Rounde which Uther, hys fadir, gaff me.'

Canto III

7   *On Benwick's beaches*: see note to I.185.

29   *Gold was Gawain, gold as sunlight.* Gawain is again likened to the sun later in the poem (III.177–9, 'the westering sun'; IV.223–4, 'the star of noon'), and 'a sun rising' was sewn on the sail of his ship (IV.142). But there is no reference to his strength increasing towards noon and then declining, which was an important element in the story of the siege of Benwick, where Lancelot wounded him grievously when his strength waned (see p.103).

55–6   These lines are a closely similar repetition of II.28–9, and reappear in the same form in another text where they are put into the mouth of Sir Lionel (p.194). Their earliest appearance is in the third synopsis, p.179.

62   *steel well-tempered:* these words have been applied to Lancelot in line 26 of this canto.

In the manuscript as written the reading was *Strong oaths she broke,* changed in pencil to *they broke*; see p.184.

68 ff. For the story here briefly suggested see pp.96 ff.

69–70 *Agravain the dour-handed* translates *Agravain a la dure mayn* (as he is called in *Sir Gawain and the Green Knight,* line 110), using *dour* in its old sense 'hard'.

82–3 *Gaheris and Gareth*: see pp.96–8.

86 Here and in line 156 the word *battle* is used in the sense 'battle array'.

89 *ruth*: remorse.

100 *little liked her*: little pleased her.

104 *bewrayed*: betrayed.

122 *siege*: seat.

140–2 These lines are a repetition of 15–16, 18 in this canto.

148 *the Lord of Logres*: King Arthur.

29   *fewte*: the track of a hunted animal. The word occurs in the accounts of the hunts in *Sir Gawain and the Green Knight*, as for example *Summe fel in þe fute þer þe fox bade*, in my father's translation (stanza 68) *Some* [of the hounds] *fell on the line to where the fox was lying.*

41   *Romeril*: Romney in Kent (see p.110).

43   A partial repetition of II.108.

68   *Leodegrance*: see note to II.198.

98–9   *the fair lily on the field sable*: see note to IV.134.

126   *sheen*: bright, shining.

126–8 According to Geoffrey of Monmouth there was painted on the inside of Arthur's shield Prydwen (see note to IV.186) an image of the Virgin Mary, so that he might never cease to think of her; and in the alliterative *Morte Arthure* the chief of Arthur's banners before the great sea-battle is thus described:

> Bot thare was chosen in the chefe a chalke-
> whitte mayden and a childe in hir arme, that
> chefe es of hevynne.

In *Sir Gawain and the Green Knight* the same is told
of Sir Gawain, who on account of his devotion to
Mary had (in my father's translation, Stanza 28)

> on the inner side of his shield her image
> depainted, that when he cast his eyes thither his
> courage never failed.

134   *flower-de-luce*, or fleur-de-lys, the heraldic lily, the
banner of Benwick (132); cf. IV.98, *the fair lily on the
field sable* [of Ban's kindred], and IV.158, *Lancelot
with his lilies came not.*

144   *a fiery griffon.* The emblem of a griffon (a beast with
the head and wings of an eagle and the body of a lion)
is ascribed to Gawain's arms in the alliterative *Morte
Arthure* (a *gryffoune of golde*: see p.119); and in notes
for the continuation of the poem beyond the point
reached (p.127) it is said that his shield bore the image
of a griffon.

146   *vaward*: vanguard.

150   *deep weighed dromonds and drawn barges.* The word
dromonds occurs in the account of the sea-battle in
the alliterative *Morte Arthure*, where Arthur's fleet
included *dromowndes* and *dragges*. In the *Oxford
English Dictionary*, where this line is cited, *dromond*
is glossed 'a very large medieval ship', while *drag*

here is defined as 'a float or raft for the conveyance of goods'.

154   *targes*: shields.

186   *Prydwen* was the name given to Arthur's shield by Geoffrey of Monmouth (see note to IV.126–8), followed by Laȝamon in the *Brut* (p.78) but in early Welsh poetry it was the name of his ship, as here.

210   *roke*: mist.

Canto V

26   *trewage*: tribute, toll.

THE POEM IN
ARTHURIAN TRADITION

THE POEM IN
ARTHURIAN TRADITION

More than seven centuries had passed since the departure
from Britain of the Roman legions when in the mid-years
of the twelfth century, probably about 1136, there appeared
a work entitled *Historia Regum Britanniae*, by Geoffrey of
Monmouth (who incidentally makes a momentary appearance
in my father's work *The Notion Club Papers*, published in
Sauron Defeated, pp.192, 216). Of this History of the Kings
of Britain it was said (by Sir Edmund Chambers, in 1927) that
'no work of imagination, save the *Aeneid*, has done more to
shape the legend of a people.' He used the word 'imagination'
advisedly. It is said that Geoffrey of Monmouth's book was the
source of the 'historical' (as opposed to the 'romance') tradition of King Arthur, but the word is very misleading unless
it is understood to mean that Geoffrey's work, while full of
marvels and extravagances embedded in a totally unhistorical
structure, was nonetheless in 'the mode of history' (a narrative chronicle of events in Latin, soberly told), but not by any
means of its substance: hence 'pseudo-historical' is a term
that is applied to it.

In this work the history of the Britons was followed through more than nineteen hundred years, and the life of King Arthur constitutes no more than a quarter of its length. 'One of the world's most brazen and successful frauds', it was called by the eminent scholar R.S. Loomis (*The Development of Arthurian Romance*, 1963). Yet he wrote also in the same place:

> The more one studies the *History of the Kings of Britain* and the methods of its composition, the more one is astonished at the author's impudence, and the more one is impressed with his cleverness, his art. Written in a polished but not ornate style, displaying sufficient harmony with learned authorities and accepted traditions, free from the wilder extravagances of the *conteurs*, founded ostensibly on a very ancient manuscript, no wonder Geoffrey's *magnum opus* disarmed scepticism and was welcomed by the learned world.

Its success and its long acceptance was a literary phenomenon of the most extraordinary nature. Of my father's own estimation of the work I have no knowledge. No doubt he would have accepted the judgement of his friend R.W. Chambers, who wrote of it that it was 'one of the most influential books ever written in this country'. He might well have been in sympathy with C.S. Lewis when he roundly condemned the Arthurian part of the work, in a posthumously published essay *The Genesis of a Medieval Book* (*Studies in Medieval and Renaissance Literature*, 1966):

Geoffrey is of course important for the historians of the Arthurian Legend; but since the interest of those historians has seldom lain chiefly in literature, they have not always remembered to tell us that he is an author of mediocre talent and no taste. In the Arthurian parts of his work the lion's share falls to the insufferable rigmarole of Merlin's prophecies and to the foreign conquests of Arthur. These latter are, of course, at once the least historical and the least mythical thing about Arthur. If there was a real Arthur he did not conquer Rome. If the story has roots in Celtic paganism, this campaign is not one of them. It is fiction. And what fiction! We can suspend our disbelief in an occasional giant or enchantress. They have friends in our subconscious and in our earliest memories; imagination can easily suppose that the real world has room for them. But vast military operations scrawled over the whole map of Europe and excluded by all the history we know are a different matter. We cannot suspend our disbelief. We don't even want to. The annals of senseless and monotonously successful aggression are dreary enough reading even when true; when blatantly, stupidly false, they are unendurable.

But from the first lines of *The Fall of Arthur* it is seen that my father was departing radically from the story of Arthur's last campaign overseas as told by Geoffrey of Monmouth and his successors. I give here a very condensed account of Geoffrey's narrative, without any discussion of such literary and traditional sources as he drew upon, since my object here is primarily to observe how *The Fall of Arthur* stands in relation to the heroic, 'chronicle' tradition initiated by him.

In his story, Arthur, on the death of his father Uther Pendragon crowned King of Britain at the age of fifteen, at once embarked on a campaign to subdue the hated and hateful Saxons, and after a number of battles the last was fought in Somerset, at Bath. Arthur bore his shield Prydwen, on which was painted an image of the Virgin Mary, his sword Caliburn which was forged in the isle of Avalon, and on his head was set a golden helmet with a crest carved in the form of a dragon. In this battle Arthur drove into the Saxon ranks, and slew with a single blow every man that he struck with Caliburn, until no less than four hundred and seventy Saxons lay dead from his hand alone.

The Saxons having fled into hiding in forests, caves and mountains, Arthur turned to the crushing of the invading Picts and Scots; and 'when he had restored the whole of the country of Britain to its ancient dignity' he married Guinevere, 'born of a noble Roman family', most beautiful of all the women of Britain. In the following year he conquered Ireland and Iceland, and the kings of Gotland and the Orkneys accepted his overlordship without a blow struck. After the passage of twelve more years Norway and Denmark were savagely put by the Britons to fire and sword and subdued to the rule of King Arthur; and all the regions of Gaul were subjected to him.

As Geoffrey of Monmouth represented him, he was now a very mighty monarch, unbeaten in battle, a name of awe throughout Europe, his knights and his household the model and pattern of chivalry and courtly life; and returning from Gaul he held in the city of Caerleon-upon-Usk in Glamorgan a high court and festival of extraordinary magnificence, from which no ruler of renown in the western lands and isles was absent. But before it ended there appeared envoys from Rome bearing a letter to Arthur from the Emperor Lucius Hiberius. In this letter Lucius demanded that Arthur should himself come to Rome to submit to judgement and punishment for the wrongs he had committed in the withholding of the tribute owing from Britain, and the seizure of lands that were tributary to the Empire; and if he did not come then Rome would move against him.

To this Arthur replied that he would indeed come to Rome, but in order to exact from the Romans the penalty that they had demanded of him. Then Lucius commanded the kings of the East to prepare their armies and to accompany him to the conquest of Britain; and the number of men in this mighty force of arms was precisely four hundred thousand and one hundred and sixty. Against them King Arthur raised a great host, and he placed the defence of Britain in his absence in the hands of his nephew Mordred and of Guinevere the Queen.

Condensing Geoffrey of Monmouth's narrative still further, and letting C.S. Lewis's words stand in place of a précis, the end of the 'Roman War' was a great victory for the Britons and the death of the Emperor Lucius; and Arthur was already in the Alps on his way to Rome when word reached him that Mordred had usurped the crown and was living adulterously with Guinevere. Here Geoffrey of Monmouth fell suddenly silent: of this matter he will say nothing, he wrote. He was as good as his word; and after the landing of King Arthur at Richborough on the coast of Kent he moved rapidly through battles with Mordred, in which Mordred and Gawain were slain and Arthur mortally wounded. Of Guinevere he said nothing save that in despair she fled to Caerleon and there became a nun; and of Arthur only that he was borne to the Isle of Avalon for the treating of his wounds. Of Sir Lancelot there is no mention at all in the *Historia Regum Britanniae*.

This was the story in the 'chronicle' or 'pseudo-historical' tradition of King Arthur deriving from Geoffrey of Monmouth: in the *Roman de Brut* of the Norman poet Wace which appeared at the time of Geoffrey's death (1155), and in the next generation the very long poem named *Brut** composed near the beginning of the thirteenth century by the Englishman Laȝamon, priest of the parish of Ernleye (Arley Regis) on the Severn in Worcestershire, following Wace but independently.

∗

---

* The name *Brut* of these and other poems derives from an old fiction, greatly elaborated by Geoffrey of Monmouth, that a certain Brutus, grandson (or great-grandson) of Aeneas of Troy, was the first man to set foot in the very desirable island of Albion (which until then was only inhabited by 'a few giants'), naming it 'Britain' from his own name, and calling his companions 'Britons'. So in the opening of *Sir Gawain and the Green Knight*, in my father's translation:
> and far over the French flood Felix Brutus
> on many a broad bank and brae Britain established
> full fair ...

The alliterative Morte Arthure

It was also the story in a work of some importance, as will be seen later, in the narrative of *The Fall of Arthur*. This is a remarkable poem of the fourteenth century 'alliterative revival' commonly known as the *alliterative Morte Arthure*. In *Sir Gawain and the Green Knight, Pearl and Sir Orfeo* (1975) I cited my father's words concerning

the ancient English measure which had descended from antiquity, that kind of verse which is now called 'alliterative'. It aimed at quite different effects from those achieved by the rhymed and syllable-counting metres derived from France and Italy; it seemed harsh and stiff and rugged to those unaccustomed to it. And quite apart from the (from a London point of view) dialectal character of the language, this 'alliterative' verse included in its diction a number of special verse words, never used in ordinary talk or prose, that were 'dark' to those outside the tradition.

In short, this poet [the author of *Sir Gawain and the Green Knight*] adhered to what is now known as the Alliterative Revival of the fourteenth century, the attempt to use the old native metre and style long rusticated for high and serious writing; and he paid the penalty for its failure, for alliterative verse was not in the event revived. The tides of time, of taste, of language, not to mention political power, trade and wealth, were against it.

The alliterative *Morte Arthure* is a long poem of over 4000 lines, of very uncertain date but commonly ascribed to the latter part of the fourteenth century, and known only from a manuscript, made by Robert Thornton, in the library of Lincoln Cathedral.* The sources of the unknown poet have been much debated, but for this purpose it is sufficient to say that in its narrative structure it derives from the *Historia Regum Britanniae* tradition. It begins with the great feast held by King Arthur to which came the envoys sent by 'Sir Lucius Iberius, the Emperour of Rome', and for much of its length it is devoted to description of Arthur's war against the Romans and their allies. It is indeed a 'heroic' poem, a *chanson de geste*, a poem of war (if by no means exclusively), of battlefields and ferocious encounters, the horrors of the sword seen with stark clarity – scenes of the Hundred Years War. A brief passage may illustrate this. Whereas Geoffrey of Monmouth told that Lucius was slain by a knight unknown, in this poem he dies at Arthur's hand, and the King's prowess is thus described:

> The emperour thane egerly   at Arthure he strykez,
> Awkwarde on the umbrere,   and egerly hym hittez!
> The nakyde swerd at the nese   noyes hym sare,
> The blode of [the] bolde kynge   over the breste rynnys,
> Beblede al the brode schelde   and the bryghte mayles!
> Oure bolde kynge bowes the blonke   by the bryghte brydylle,

---

* My father used a copy of the Early English Text Society edition, as revised by Edmund Brock, 1871, which he acquired in September 1919, and which I have used for the quotations in this book.

With his burlyche brande   a buffette hym reches,
Thourghe the brene and the breste   with his bryghte wapyne,
O-slante doune fro the slote   he slyttes at ones!
Thus endys the emperour   of Arthure hondes ...*

After the death of the Emperor in the last great battle of
the war against the Romans the alliterative *Morte Arthure*
extends for many hundreds of lines in accounts of further
aggressive campaigns led by Arthur, not found in Geoffrey
of Monmouth, until we find the King north of Rome in the
vale of Viterbo 'among the vines', and 'was never meriere
men made on this erthe'.

To Arthur in this very agreeable place there came envoys
from Rome to sue for peace, among them the 'konyngeste
cardynalle that to the courte lengede' [belonged], who
brought a proposal that the Pope should crown him in Rome
as sovereign and lord. King Arthur now gloried in the splendour of his success, and saying that Rome is now ours, and
that he will be crowned there at Christmas, he took himself,
being weary from lack of sleep, to bed.

But be ane aftyre mydnyghte   alle his mode changede;
He mett in the morne-while   fulle mervaylous dremes!

---

* *Awkwarde on the umbrere* with a back stroke (?) on the visor;
nese nose; *noyes hym sare* grieves him sore; *Beblede* made bloody;
mayles chain-mail; *bowes the blonke* turns the horse; *burlyche
brande* stout sword; *brene* cuirass; *O-slante* aslant; *slote* hollow
above the breast-bone.

And when his dredefulle drem was drefene to the ende,
The kynge dares for dowte, dye as he scholde;
Sendes aftyre phylosophers, and his affraye telles.*

I have said that the alliterative *Morte Arthure* is a heroic
poem celebrating Arthur, above all a poem of battles; but
when it is far advanced one becomes aware that it was only
with Arthur's dream amid the vineyards of the valley of
Viterbo that the author's large design was to be fulfilled. That
dream, as he described it to his 'philosophers' when he awoke
in fear, was an elaborate and ornate vision of the Wheel of
Fortune, on which are set eight of the 'Nine Worthies' or
'Nine Heroes', the great rulers and conquerors of history: of
this I give here a very abbreviated account.

He dreamed that he was alone and lost in a forest full of
wolves and wild boars, and lions that lapped up the blood
of his faithful knights; but fleeing away he found himself in
a mountain meadow, 'the meryeste of medillerthe that men
myghte beholde', and saw descending out of the clouds a god-
dess in magnificent garments, the embodiment of Fortune,
bearing in her hands a wheel made of gold and silver which
she whirled about in her white hands. Arthur saw that there
was 'a chayere of chalke-whytte silver' at the top of Fortune's
Wheel, from which six kings had fallen and now clung with
broken crowns to the outer circle of the wheel, each in turn

---

*   *ane* one; *mode* mood, mind; *mett* dreamed; *dares for dowte* lies
still for fear; *dye as he scholde* as if he were about to die; *affraye*
fear.

lamenting that he had fallen from such heights of greatness and power; and two kings were climbing up to claim the high seat at the summit of the wheel. The lady Fortune now raised Arthur to that seat, telling him that it was through her that he had won all his honour in war, that she had chosen him to sit in the high chair, and treating him as 'soverayne in erthe'. But suddenly 'at midday' her manner changed towards him, saying 'Thow has lyffede in delytte and lordchippes inewe' [enough], and 'abowte scho whirles the whele, and whirles me undire', so that all his body was crushed; and he awoke.

The philosopher who interpreted his dream told him in hard words that he was at the high point of his fortune, and now must fall from it.

> Thow has schedde myche blode,   and schalkes distroyede,
> Sakeles, in cirquytrie,   in sere kynges landis;
> Schryfe the of thy schame,   and schape for thyne ende!
> Thow has a schewynge,   sir kynge, take kepe yif the lyke,
> For thow sall fersely falle   within fyve wynters!*

And having expounded at length the meaning of what King Arthur had seen in his sleep, the learned man declared that the wild beasts in the wood were wicked men that had entered his land to harass his people, and warned him that within ten days he would hear tidings that some mischief

---

* *schalkes* men; *Sakeles* guiltless; *cirquytrie* arrogance; *sere* various, many; *Schryfe the* confess; *schape* prepare; *schewynge* vision; *take kepe yif the lyke* take heed if you will; *fersely* violently.

had befallen in Britain since his departure. He called on the king to repent his unjust deeds, to 'amend his mood' (that is, to change his disposition) and meekly ask for mercy ere misfortune befall him.

Then Arthur arose and having dressed (seven lines are devoted to a close description of his magnificent attire) set off to walk alone; and at sunrise he met with a man in the humble clothes (to which as many lines are devoted) that marked him as a pilgrim, on his way to Rome. Accosting him Arthur learned that he was Sir Cradoc, and known to him as 'a knight of his chamber, the keeper of Caerleon'. In Geoffrey of Monmouth's story it is not told how Arthur heard of the treachery of Mordred, but in the poem it was the express purpose of Sir Cradoc's journey (and it was Sir Cradoc who brought the news in *The Fall of Arthur*, I.145). He told that Mordred had crowned himself King of Britain, taken castles, prepared a great fleet lying off Southampton, brought in Danes and Saxons, Picts and Saracens to rule the realm, and worst of all his deeds had wedded Guinevere and begotten a child.

From this point the narrative of the alliterative *Morte Arthur* continues for some eight hundred lines. To this, and its relation to *The Fall of Arthur*, I will return (pp.116 ff.).

✻

It is a notable feature of English Arthurian history that Sir Thomas Malory's fifth book (in Caxton's numbering), *The Tale of the Noble King Arthur that was Emperor Himself,* was very closely based on the alliterative *Morte Arthure* (and on no other source): he had the manuscript before him as he made his very judicious prose rendering (but he had access to a manuscript more authentic in detail than that at Lincoln written by Robert Thornton).

Professor Eugène Vinaver, in his great edition (*The Works of Sir Thomas Malory*, three volumes, 1947), showed that this tale was actually the first that Malory wrote, and he argued that 'contrary to the generally accepted view, he first became familiar with the Arthurian legend not through "French books" but through an English poem, the alliterative *Morte Arthure*' (Vinaver, I, xli).

With well over a thousand lines of the alliterative *Morte Arthure* still to go, Malory nevertheless abruptly abandoned it, at the point where Arthur, encamped near Viterbo, received the Roman envoys who came seeking peace, with the offer of coronation by the Pope. From here Malory sped rapidly to the end of his tale. Arthur was duly crowned as Emperor, and soon afterwards he returned to Britain. He landed at Sandwich on the coast of Kent, and 'whan quene Guenyvere herde of his commynge she mette with hym at London'. At the beginning of the tale Malory omitted all reference to Arthur's appointment of his nephew Mordred as regent in his absence; and now at its end he rejected the entire story of Mordred's treachery, Guinevere's adultery, and Arthur's downfall. With it of course went the dream of the Wheel of Fortune. When he wrote this tale Malory had no interest in the representation of the tale of King Arthur as the tragedy of an overweening hero.

It will be seen that in the first canto of *The Fall of Arthur* my father was preserving the essential narrative idea of the 'chronicle' or 'pseudo-historical' tradition, the great expedition of King Arthur eastwards over the sea. But his poem enters at once *in medias res*, without any introductory setting or immediate motive:

> Arthur eastward   in arms purposed
> his war to wage   on the wild marches,

for

> So fate fell-woven   forward drave him.

The great feast, going back to Geoffrey of Monmouth, held at Caerleon to celebrate Arthur's victories, is absent, and with it the coming of the Roman envoys with the menacing letter from the Emperor, which provided the motive for the last campaign of the King of the Britons. In *The Fall of Arthur* there is no trace of this conception. So far from being the zenith of his life's attainment as the conqueror who beat down the Roman armies and had Rome's emissaries begging for peace, his purpose was to 'ward off ruin from the Roman realm' (I.4).

The aims and extent of the campaign are in fact somewhat obscure. At first it is clear that Arthur's intent was to assail the Saxon pirates in their own lairs, and it seems reasonable to suppose therefore that 'the Roman realm' which he will defend against them must surely be the realm of Roman Britain; but a larger horizon seems to me to be suggested by the references to Mirkwood (I.68, 132). I cannot say whether

my father intended a more precise meaning in his use of this
ancient legendary name for a dark boundary forest separating
peoples, but since Arthur's host marched 'from the mouths
of the Rhine / o'er many kingdoms' (I.43), and rode 'ever
east and onward' (I.62), and since the forest of Mirkwood lay
'on the houseless hills ever higher mounting / vast, unvanquished' (I.70–1) it seems that they were now far to the east
of the regions of Saxon settlement; and this is strongly borne
out by Sir Cradoc's words (I.153–4): 'While war ye wage on
the wild peoples / in the homeless East ...'

It is also remarkable that in the hundred lines of the first
Canto of the poem from the beginning of Arthur's expedition at line 39 to the coming of Sir Cradoc with his evil
tidings there is (beside 'Foes before them, flames behind
them', I.61) only one reference to the destruction of heathen
habitations by the invading host (I.41–3):

Halls and temples   of the heathen kings
his might assailed   marching in conquest
from the mouths of the Rhine   o'er many kingdoms.

My father seems intent rather on conveying a hostile and wintry
world of storms and ice, of 'ravens croaking among ruinous
rocks', unpeopled save by 'phantom foes with fell voices' and
wolves howling, a menacing world in which (I.134–6)

Fear clutched their souls,
waiting watchful   in a world of shadow
for woe they knew not,   no word speaking.

Moreover, this sense of vast impending danger accompanies the assertions of the poet that the declared purpose of Arthur is a matter of the gravest consequence, a great heroic gamble against fate:

> Thus the tides of time   to turn backward
> and the heathen to humble,   his hope urged him (I.5–6)

– echoed in lines I.176–9, after receiving the news of Mordred's treachery:

> Now from hope's summit   headlong falling
> his heart foreboded   that his house was doomed,
> the ancient world   to its end falling
> and the tides of time   turned against him.

So also, Gawain leading the host 'as in last sortie from leaguered city' is

> defence and fortress   of a falling world. (I.55)

And later (II.147–9) Mordred knows that

> Time is changing;
> the West waning,   a wind rising
> in the waxing East.   The world falters.

It is surely the fall of Rome and Roman Christendom that they see approaching in 'the tides of time'.

But however these aspects of *The Fall of Arthur* are interpreted, it is clear that Arthur's great expedition to the Continent, while as equally without root in history as the assault on Roman power of Geoffrey of Monmouth and his successors, is set more nearly within the historical circumstances from which the Arthurian legend arose: the struggle of the Britons in the fifth century against the Germanic invaders. In *The Fall of Arthur* the mark of the enemy is that he is heathen. This is the fate of the Frisian sea-captain who brought to Mordred the news of Arthur's return to Britain (II.89–93):

Radbod the red,   rover fearless,
heathen-hearted   to hate faithful,
died as his doom was.   Dark was the morning.
To sea they cast him,   of his soul recked not
that walks in the waters,   wandering homeless.

He 'passed to hell' (II.67). Thus the heathen barbarians are dispatched to inevitable perdition in the metre that the barbarians brought to the conquered lands. *Wild blow the winds of war in Britain!* says Sir Cradoc, when telling King Arthur (I.160) of the heathen dragon ships driving in on the unguarded shores; and five centuries later Torhthelm, in *The Homecoming of Beorhtnoth*, repeats his words with reference to the Norsemen:

So the last is fallen   of the line of earls,
from Saxon lords   long-descended,

89

who sailed the seas,   as songs tell us,
from Angel in the east,   with eager swords
upon war's anvil   the Welsh smiting.
Realms here they won   and royal kingdoms,
and in olden days   this isle conquered.
And now from the North   need comes again:
wild blows the wind   of war to Britain!

A distinctive feature of the first canto of *The Fall of Arthur* concerns Mordred, who at the very outset of the narrative is portrayed as in his 'malice' sustaining King Arthur in his resolve to carry war into the lands of the barbarous peoples, for a hidden purpose lay beneath his words (I.27–9):

And Britain the blessed,   thy broad kingdom,
I will hold unharmed   till thy home-coming.
Faithful hast thou found me.

Where Geoffrey of Monmouth devoted no more than a single sentence to the matter ('He made over the task of defending Britain to his nephew Mordred and his Queen Guinevere'), in the alliterative *Morte Arthure* the king is remarkably long-winded in his exposition of the burden – and Mordred begs (unsuccessfully) to be excused from it and to be allowed to accompany Arthur to the war. There is no hint of what is to come. In *The Fall of Arthur* it is said that Sir Gawain had no inkling of 'guile or treason' in Mordred's 'bold counsel', for (I.36–8)

> he was for battle eager,
> in idle ease   the evil seeing
> that had rent asunder   the Round Table.

With these words my father introduced an element into the narrative that sets it altogether apart from works in the 'chronicle' tradition. A few lines later (I.44–5) it is said that Lancelot and other knights were not with Arthur in his campaign, and later in the first Canto, after he had heard the news of Mordred's treason from Sir Cradoc, King Arthur consulted with Sir Gawain (I.180 ff.) and told him how greatly he missed Sir Lancelot and 'the mighty swords of Ban's kindred', and thought it the wisest course to send to Lancelot's people and ask their aid. From this Sir Gawain sternly dissented.

None of this is comprehensible as it stands, and it may well be that my father anticipated some familiarity on the reader's part with the story of Lancelot and Guinevere. The causes of the estrangement between Arthur and Lancelot do indeed appear in the third canto of the poem, but in a very oblique fashion.

It would lie far outside my intention here to enter into any account of the 'strains' or 'streams' of mediaeval Arthurian legend, the 'pseudo-historical' or 'chronicle' tradition on the one hand, and the vast 'romantic' development of the 'Matter of Britain' in French prose and poetry. I am concerned solely to indicate the characteristics of my father's treatment of the legend of Lancelot and Guinevere.

I have noticed already that in Geoffrey of Monmouth's *Historia Regum Britanniae* there is no mention whatever of Sir

Lancelot. In the alliterative *Morte Arthure* he does appear several times, but in almost every case he is named merely as one among the chief knights of the Round Table.* Of his appearance in Malory's *Tale of the Noble King Arthur that was Emperor Himself* (see p.84 above) Professor Vinaver observed:

> Malory's account gives the impression that Lancelot is nothing but a warrior, and that all his great qualities of mind and heart are to be placed for ever in the service of his king. No reader [of Malory's Tale] would gather from it that Lancelot had been from the very beginning a courtly hero, that he had first appeared in medieval romance as a champion of *courtoisie*, and that it was as the protagonist of Chrétien de Troyes' *Conte de la Charette*† that he had

---

* Very oddly he is the slayer of the Emperor Lucius, although less than 200 lines later Lucius is slain again by King Arthur (verses cited above, pp.80–1).

† The reference is to the *Lancelot* of the French poet of the later twelfth century Chrétien de Troyes, a work known also as *Le Chevalier de la Charette, The Knight of the Cart*. The name derives from an incident in the narrative in which Lancelot, the secret and impassioned lover of Queen Guinevere, set out to rescue her from captivity in the land of the prince Meleagant. Having lost his horse he accepted the offer of a dwarvish carter to be carried forward on his vital errand: but the cart was a tumbril, used to carry malefactors as a public spectacle to the place of execution. Lancelot thus showed himself ready to submit to the extremity of disgrace and ignominy in the eyes of the courtly world for the sake of Guinevere. That he hesitated momentarily before stepping into the cart of shame was held against him by his idolized lady, a defect in his absolute subservience to the code of *amour courtois*.

won his world-wide fame. It was because Lancelot had only been known as a courtly knight that he had had so few attractions for earlier English writers: they had found little in him to support and illustrate their epic treatment of Arthurian romance. The author of the [alliterative] *Morte Arthure*, no doubt for this very reason, had relegated Lancelot to comparative insignificance. Malory's attitude was at first much the same: his mind, like that of his English predecessors, dwelled on problems of human heroism, not on the subtle issues of courtly behaviour. And in order to restore Lancelot to fame he made him into a genuine epic hero, more akin to the Gawain of the *Morte Arthure* than to Chrétien's 'knight of the cart'. We do not know how much of the French tradition was directly accessible to him when he wrote his *Tale of Arthur and Lucius*. What is certain is that he was then primarily an epic writer, unwilling and perhaps even unable to follow the romanticized knight-errantry and understand its fascination. The great adventure of the French books had not yet begun.

Of Lancelot in *The Fall of Arthur*, introduced in so allusive a way, it can be said at once that he is no fantastic figure out of 'romanticized knight-errantry'; and the source of the story that he was introducing is not doubtful. In the French romance in prose entitled the *Mort Artu*, the theme of the adulterous love of Sir Lancelot and Queen Guinevere was combined with that of the treason of Mordred and the fall of King Arthur. The *Mort Artu* was the source for an English poem of the fourteenth century named *Le Morte Arthur*, commonly referred to as the *stanzaic Morte Arthur* (to distinguish it from the *alliterative Morte Arthure*), a long poem of nearly 4000 lines composed in eight-line stanzas. Sir Thomas Malory made use of both the *Mort Artu* and the English poem, closely consulting and comparing them to provide the narrative structure on which he founded his last book, *The Morte Arthur* properly so called.*

✳

The stanzaic Morte Arthur and Malory's Tale of the Death of Arthur

I shall here recount Malory's narrative in brief, but before doing so I will cite a few stanzas of the English poem from the beginning of the final tragedy to give some indication of its manner and form.

> A tyme befelle, sothe to sayne,
> The knyghtis stode in chambyr and spake,
> Both Gaheriet, and syr Gawayne,

---

* Malory ended his tale with these words: 'Here is the ende of the hoole [*whole*] book of kyng Arthur and of his noble knyghtes of the Rounde Table. ... And here is the ende of *The Deth of Arthur*.' William Caxton took the last sentence to refer to the whole compilation of Malory's Arthurian tales, and ended the text of his edition of 1485 with the words 'Thus endeth thys noble and Ioyous book entytled le morte Darthur'.

And Mordreite, that mykelle couthe of wrake;
'Allas,' than sayde syr Agrawayne,
'How fals men schalle we us make,
And how longe shalle we hele and layne
The treson of Launcelote du Lake!

Wele we wote, wythouten wene,
The kynge Arthur oure eme sholde be,
And Launcelote lyes by the quene;
Ageyne the kynge trator is he,
And that wote alle the curte bydene,
And iche day it here and see:
To the kynge we shulde it mene,
Yif ye wille do by the counselle of me.'

'Wele wote we,' sayd sir Gawayne,
'That we are of the kyngis kynne,
And Launcelot is so mykylle of mayne,
That suche wordys were better blynne;
Welle wote thou, brothyr Agrawayne,
Thereof shulde we bot harmys wynne;
Yit were it better to hele and layne,
Than werre and wrake thus to begynne.*

---

* *mykelle* much; *couthe* knew; *wrake* trouble, harm, ruin; *hele and layne* hide and conceal; *wene* doubt; *eme* uncle; *bydene* together; *mene* tell; *mayne* strength; *blynne* left (unsaid). In the first of these stanzas *Gaheriet* is the form in the *Mort Artu* and the stanzaic *Morte Arthur* of the name of Gawain's brother Gareth, as he is named by Malory and in *The Fall of Arthur* (III.82).

The first scene, the matter of these stanzas, is thus introduced by Malory:

hit befelle in the moneth of May a grete angur and unhappy
[*disastrous*] that stynted nat tylle the floure of chyvalry of
the worlde was destroyed and slayne. And all was longe
uppon [*due to*] two unhappy [*pernicious*] knyghtis whych
were named sir Aggravayne and sir Mordred, that were
brethirn unto sir Gawayne. For thys sir Aggravayne and
sir Mordred had ever a prevy hate unto the quene, dame
Gwenyver, and to sir Launcelot; and dayly and nyghtly
they ever wacched uppon sir Launcelot.

It happened that Gawain and his brothers Agravain, Gareth,
and Gaheris (the sons of Arthur's sister Morgause and king Lot
of Lothian), and also Mordred (who in the tradition followed
by Malory was the son by unwitting incest of Arthur and
Morgause[*]), met together in King Arthur's chamber. Agravain
declared that it was known to everyone 'how sir Launcelot
lyeth dayly and nyghtly by the quene', and that he intended
to inform on Lancelot to the king. To this Gawain, being
himself devoted to Lancelot, most illustrious of the knights
of the Round Table, was profoundly opposed, foreseeing the
likelihood of disastrous strife, as were his brothers Gareth and

---

[*]   So in the stanzaic *Morte Arthur*:
          That fals traytour, Sir Mordreid,
          The kynges sister sone he was,
          And eke his owne sone, as I rede.

Gaheris also; and after blunt words they left the chamber as King Arthur entered, demanding to know what was toward. And when Agravain told him, he was greatly troubled, for although he had a suspicion of the truth he had no wish to pursue the matter against so great a man as Lancelot. He said therefore that he would do nothing without the proof that could only be had if Lancelot were taken in the act.

To this end Agravain proposed the setting of a trap. The king should ride out hunting on the next day, and he should send word to the queen that he would not return that night. Then Agravain and Mordred and twelve other knights would go to her chamber and bring back Lancelot alive or dead. But this did not befall. When Lancelot was with the queen the fourteen knights came to the door and with high words Agravain and Mordred called him out as a traitor; but Lancelot was wholly without armour and weapons, and he and the queen were in great distress. Then Lancelot unbarred the chamber-door and opened it only so far as to let one man pass through; and when Sir Colgrevance did so and struck at him with his sword Lancelot felled him with a single blow. Then he put on the dead man's armour, and striding out among the other knights he slew without hurt to himself all of them, including two sons of Gawain and his brother Agravain, save Mordred, who was wounded and fled away.

When the king learned of all this from Mordred he foresaw that the fellowship of the Round Table was broken for ever, for many knights would hold with Lancelot; but Guinevere must 'have the law', and he commanded that the queen be taken to the fire and there to be burnt. Gawain ardently urged Arthur to be less hasty in passing this judgement, pleading the possibility that Lancelot had gone to the queen in all innocence, but the king was adamant. He said that if he laid hands on Lancelot he should die as shameful a death, and why should this trouble Sir Gawain since he had slain his brother and his sons? To this Gawain replied that he had warned them of their peril, and that they had brought about their own deaths. But the king was unmoved, and ordered Gawain with his brothers Gareth and Gaheris to put on their armour and bring the queen to the fire. Gawain refused the command of King Arthur. Then let Sir Gareth and Sir Gaheris be present, said the king. They were unable to refuse, but said that they would go to the burning greatly against their will, and that they would wear no armour. Then Gawain wept bitterly, and said 'Alas, that ever I shulde endure to se this wofull day!'

Now Lancelot with a great number of armed knights, who supported him and his determination to rescue the queen if she were condemned, were waiting in a wood at no great distance, and when it was reported that the queen was about to die they raced to the place of the burning and a fierce battle arose. Lancelot hewing to right and left at all who withstood him smote two men who were 'unarmed and unwares' and 'he saw them nat'; but they were Gawain's brothers Gareth and Gaheris, and Gawain had extraordinary devotion to Gareth, as did Gareth to Lancelot.

Lancelot went to Guinevere where she stood, and setting her on his horse he rode with her to his castle of Joyous

Garde, and they remained there. King Arthur fell into an extremity of grief at these events. He ordered that no one should tell Gawain:

> 'for I am sure,' seyde the kynge, 'whan he hyryth telle that sir Gareth is dede he wyll go nygh oute of hys mynde'. 'Merci Jesu,' seyde the kynge, 'why slew he sir Gaherys and sir Gareth? For I dare sey, as for sir Gareth, he loved sir Launcelot of all men erthly.'

The death of his brothers, said the king, will cause the greatest mortal war that ever was. For Gawain of course soon learned of it; and he was changed in a short space from Lancelot's devoted friend to his implacable foe. In the words of the stanzaic *Morte Arthur* he cried out:

> Betwixte me and Launcelote du Lake
> Nys man in erthe, for sothe to sayne,
> Shall trewes sette and pees make
> Er outher of vs haue other slayne.

Or as he said to the king in Malory's tale: 'For I promyse unto God, for the deth of my brothir Sir Gareth, I shall seke sir Launcelot thorowoute seven kynges realmys, but I shall sle hym, other ellis he shall sle me.'

To which King Arthur replied: 'Sir, ye shall nat nede to seke hym so far, for as I here say, sir Launcelot woll abyde me and us all wythin the castell of Joyous Garde.'

Then the king with Sir Gawain at the head of a great host laid siege to Joyous Garde. Much time passed before Sir Lancelot would issue from the castle with his knights, but at last he appeared on the walls and spoke to Arthur and Gawain below, replying to their verbal assault in conciliatory words, seeking to avoid conflict of arms with them, and most especially with the king. He spoke of the many dangers that he had rescued them from, asserted his wholly unwitting slaying of Sir Gareth and Sir Gaheris, the perfect innocence of Guinevere, and the rightness of his rescue of her from the burning. But all this was to no avail, and a great battle arose at Joyous Garde, in which Lancelot went so far in his refusal to return the attempted blows of King Arthur, who was 'ever about sir Launcelot to have slain him', that he raised him up when he had been unhorsed by Sir Bors de Ganis and set him on his horse again.

After two days of fierce fighting, in which Gawain was wounded, the hosts separated, that of Sir Lancelot being now in the ascendant; and at this time there came to King Arthur an envoy from Rome bearing an edict of the Pope, charging him that on pain of an interdict on all England he must receive back the queen and come to an accord with Sir Lancelot.

Lancelot did all in his power to further the Papal demand. He brought back Guinevere to the king; but against the coldly implacable hatred of Gawain he could not prevail. The end of it was banishment, and he departed from the court in bitterness, saying, in Malory's tale:

Most nobelyst Crysten realme, whom I have loved aboven all other realmys! And in the I have gotyn a grete parte of my worshyp [*honour*], and now that I shall departe in thys wyse, truly me repentis that ever I cam in thys realme, that I shulde be thus shamefully banysshyd, undeserved and causeles! But fortune is so varyaunte, and the wheele so mutable, that there ys no constaunte abydynge.

But Gawain said:

Wyte thou well we shall sone com aftir, and breke the strengyst castell that thou hast, uppon thy hede!

In the stanzaic *Morte Arthur* Lancelot asked that he should be safe from pursuit in his own lands in France, but:

Syr Gawayne than sayd, 'naye,
By hym that made sonne and mone,
Dight the as welle as euyr thou may,
For we shalle after come fulle sone.'

Then Lancelot said farewell to Guinevere and he kissed her, and then he said 'all opynly':

'Now lat se whatsomever he be in thys place that dare say the queen ys nat trew unto my lorde Arthur, lat se who woll speke and [*if*] he dare speke.' And therewith he brought the quene to the kynge, and than sir Launcelot toke hys leve and departed. ...

And so he toke his way to Joyous Garde, and than ever afftir he called hit the 'Dolerous Garde'. And thus departed sir Launcelot frome the courte for ever.

Then he gathered many knights about him and they took ship for France.

Sir Lancelot was the son of King Ban, who ruled over a city and a realm in France named, both in the stanzaic *Morte Arthur* and in Malory, *Benwick*; in the *Mort Artu* it is *Benoic.* Some of the Knights of the Round Table were close kin of Lancelot, among them Sir Ector de Maris (his brother), Sir Lionel, Sir Bors de Ganis, and Sir Blamore de Ganis (these knights are named in *The Fall of Arthur*, I.44–5, and again in III.131–2). Thus the destination of these exiles was Benwick; but where it was thought to be has not, to my knowledge, been discovered. Malory said at this point in his tale that they 'sayled unto Benwyke: som men calle hit Bayan and some men calle hit Beawme, where the wyne of Beawme ys.' But no such identification is made elsewhere; and since Benwick is clearly a port, it cannot be Beaune, which is many hundreds of miles from the Atlantic; while if *Bayan* is Bayonne, that is very far to the south.

But wherever Benwick was, it was not long before King Arthur and Sir Gawain, the leading spirit in the enterprise, carried out his threat. The king 'made sir Mordred chyeff ruler of all Ingelonde, and also he put the quene undir hys governunace', and with a great host they crossed the sea, and began to burn and lay waste Sir Lancelot's lands. Still striving for peace, despite the opinion among his knights that 'youre curtesy woll shende [*ruin*] us all', Lancelot sent to King Arthur, but again received the response, that the king 'wolde acccord with sir Launcelot, but sir Gawayne woll nat suffir hym'. Then at the gate of the besieged town of Benwick Gawain appeared and cried out a challenge to the defenders. Sir Bors and then Sir Lionel rode against him, but both were badly worsted and hurt, and so it went on until at last and reluctantly Lancelot took up the challenge.

In all the accounts of this war Sir Gawain is credited with the possession of a very singular 'grace', a faculty whereby his strength greatly increased towards noon and then again declined. When Lancelot perceived that this was so he dodged to and fro and avoided Gawain's thrusts for a long time until his miraculous strength began to wane, whereupon Lancelot fell on him and gave him a great wound. (Incidentally the *Mort Artu* tells the story that during the time of Gawain's recovery Arthur left the siege of Benwick and conducted his Roman campaign, in which the Emperor Lucius was slain; Malory of course ignored this, since he had already told the story in his tale of Arthur and the Emperor Lucius, p.84 above.) But when Gawain was able to fight again all was repeated a second time with the same outcome, for Lancelot struck him in the place of the former wound. And even yet Gawain's hatred was unappeased, but as he prepared for a third attempt news came from England that led Arthur to raise the siege of Benwick and return. That news was that Mordred had claimed to have received letters telling that Arthur had been slain in battle by Lancelot; that he had 'made a parlemente', and had had himself crowned king at Canterbury; and that he had declared that he would wed Guinevere, naming the day and preparing the bridal feast.

To Mordred Guinevere masked her intention, but fled to London and took refuge from him in the Tower; and though he attacked it he could not take it, and there she remained. But now Arthur with a great navy was approaching Dover, and there was Mordred awaiting him.

*

Thus it had been brought about that while King Arthur's seaborne campaign remained the precedent history had entirely changed. It was the love of Lancelot and Guinevere that in a long chain of causation brought the king's departure from England (not 'Britain') to pass: from the intrusion of Agravain and Mordred to the death by burning imposed on Guinevere, from which Lancelot rescued her, but at the cost of his slaying of Gareth and Gaheris, whereby Gawain's love of Lancelot is changed to insane hatred, to the banishment of Lancelot, and so to the expedition of vengeance against him in his lands in France. Congruence between the distinct traditions, exemplified by the alliterative *Morte Arthure* and the stanzaic *Morte Arthur,* is only reached when news reaches Arthur overseas of Mordred's usurpation of the kingdom.

It will be seen that in many features the third canto of *The Fall of Arthur* is much at variance, largely by omission, with Malory's *Tale of the Death of Arthur* (as also with the stanzaic *Morte Arthur*). There is no suggestion that Lancelot's killing of Gawain's brothers was the crucial moment in the development of the tragedy; and it is certainly the case that what is vital to the story in the old versions, the relentless hatred felt for Lancelot by Gawain, his former devoted friend, is absent. In Canto III Gawain appears only (lines 29 ff.) in a portrait, expressly juxtaposed, to his advantage, with that of Lancelot which precedes it, and again in a reference (III.177 ff.) to his glory while Lancelot in Benwick 'over leagues of sea / looked and pondered alone musing / doubtful-hearted'. But he plays no part in the narrative until the sea-battle on Arthur's return. It is true that in Canto I Gawain, speaking 'grave and slowly', opposes Arthur's desire to call upon Lancelot and his people for aid against Mordred (I.190 ff.); but it seems that Gawain's dissent arose from doubt of the loyalty of 'Ban's kindred', and the measured tone of his words is far removed from the implacable anger of the Gawain of the old books.

In *The Fall of Arthur* the narrative of events following Guinevere's rescue from the fire is reduced to the words 'far he bore her; / fear fell on men, none would follow after' (III.83–4); and the entire story of the siege of Joyous Garde by Arthur and Gawain, the fierce fighting there, the intensity of Lancelot's chivalric loyalty to the king, the intervention of the Pope – all this has gone.

The conception, in the retrospective view of Canto III, of the breaking of the fellowship of the Round Table and the complexity of Lancelot's loves and loyalties is thus rendered far simpler. With the absence of Gawain a dimension is removed. The gulf that opened between King Arthur and

Sir Lancelot becomes more sharply defined, and is found to be impossible of resolution. This is clearly stated more than once:

> He his lord betrayed   to love yielding,
> and love forsaking   lord regained not;
> faith was refused him   who had faith broken,
> by leagues of sea   from love sundered.
> (III.15–18, repeated without the third line in III.140–2.)

The rescue of Guinevere from the stake remains crucial in *The Fall of Arthur*, but not on account of the slaying of Gareth and Gaheris: rather it is on account of the reckless violence of Lancelot's irruption on the scene, which was followed by a Túrin-like subsidence after a great rage, and led to a far-reaching penitence of spirit and attempt to undo the havoc he had caused, an agonizing recognition of guilt.

> His pride he repented, his prowess cursing
> that friends had felled, faith had broken. (III.90–1)

Above all, 'Strong oaths they broke' (III.62): he must restore Guinevere to the king, seeking his mercy towards her and his own reacceptance.

Neither in the stanzaic *Morte Arthur* nor in Malory's tale is there any reference to Guinevere's thoughts or wishes in the matter. Very different is her treatment in *The Fall of Arthur*, where her desires are analyzed, and where she finds this new Lancelot an unwelcome stranger whose disturbance of mind she cannot comprehend: 'Strange she deemed him, / by a sudden sickness from his self altered' (III.95–6). The same words are used of Lancelot: 'Strange he deemed her / from her self altered'. But Lancelot's loss was far greater than Guinevere's; for 'Though in wrath she left him, no ruth show-ing, / proud and scornful, dear he loved her' (III.166–8). 'In the courts of Camelot she was queen again, / great and glori-ous' (III.113–14); while Lancelot as petitioner was by King Arthur rejected utterly, and banished to his dark reflections in another land. But the king, sad at heart, knew that he had lost the best of all his knights and many with him; and while he lamented this to Gawain when the news of Mordred's treason reached them (I.180 ff.), Lancelot in Benwick, hear-ing rumours of approaching war, turned over in his mind conflicting thoughts of Arthur and Guinevere (III.143 ff.).

With the absence of Gawain, the invasion of Benwick which he inspired in vengeance against Lancelot also disap-peared in *The Fall of Arthur*. We do not see Arthur again until Canto IV, when Mordred on the sea-cliffs hears the cry of 'A sail, a sail on the sea shining!' (IV.117). But before the 'Lancelot story' enters in retrospective form in Canto III there is the wholly original Canto II, in which is told how the dying captain of a ship wrecked on the coast, a heathen sea-rover named Radbod in the pay of Mordred, reported to him that Sir Cradoc (as told in Canto I) had slipped out of Britain and followed the trail of King Arthur to warn him of the designs of Mordred against him; already Arthur was hastening back to Britain. With his last breath Radbod gave

Mordred a tense account of the feverish preparations of warriors and ships (II.76–89).

But the most remarkable aspect of Canto II of *The Fall of Arthur* is the emergence of Mordred as a fully imagined figure in the approaching calamity.

In Canto I no more has been told of him than that his vigorous support of Arthur's eastward campaign veiled a secret and evil purpose which is now revealed. Guinevere has not been named. Of his association with the queen Geoffrey of Monmouth had said only (p.77 above) that after his victory over the Romans news reached King Arthur that she was living adulterously with Mordred. In the alliterative *Morte Arthure* (p.84) Sir Cradoc told the king that 'worst of all Mordred's deeds he had wedded Guinevere and begotten a child'. In Malory's version of the story (p.104) the news that reached Arthur at Benwick was that Mordred had declared that he would wed Guinevere. In full Malory's text reads:

And so he made redy for the feste, and a day prefyxte that they shulde be wedded; wherefore quene Gwenyver was passyng hevy. But she durst nat discover her harte, but spake fayre, and aggreed to sir Mordredys wylle. And anone she desyred of sir Mordred to go to London to byghe [*buy*] all maner thynges that longed to the brydale. And bycause of her fayre speche sir Mordred trusted her and gaff her leve; and so whan she cam to London she toke the Towre of London, and suddeynly in all haste possyble she stuffed hit with all maner of vytayle, and wel garnysshed hit with men, and so kepte hit.

In Canto I of *The Fall of Arthur* Sir Cradoc says nothing of Guinevere; but in Canto II before Radbod the ship's captain had delivered his tidings Mordred is seen looking out from a high window indifferent to the storm in which the ship foundered (II.18–31), for his mind was wholly absorbed in his desire for Guinevere; and when he had heard what Radbod had to tell, and had sent 'messengers speeding / northward and eastward the news bearing', he set out for Camelot. Guinevere heard the quick steps of this deeply sinister man as he came up the stair to her bower. At that fateful meeting Mordred offered her a choice that was no choice, between 'slave or lady, wife or captive' (II.154–5). Guinevere asked for time, but he would grant her little enough: 'twixt bride and bond / brief be the choosing!' She decided on immediate flight - but not to the Tower of London. She stole away in a dark cloak; and we see next the lights of Camelot fading behind her as she fled westward with a few companions, making for the castle of King Leodogrance, her father.

Canto II ends with her thoughts of Lancelot: would he return? Canto IV begins with a bright morning on the borders of Wales, when the riders sent out by Mordred to hunt her down lose all trace of her.

> The queen they hunted   with cold hatred,
> till their hope failed them   amid houseless stones,
> halting hungry-eyed   under the hills' menace
> at the walls of Wales.

Then follows the news of their failure delivered to Mordred by his squire Ivor, together with some advice out of season that enraged his master, as he stood in his camp on the coastal cliffs above Romeril (Romney in Kent), gazing at the empty sea: fearful lest Guinevere had sent a messenger to Lancelot, 'love recalling /and his aid asking in her evil day' (IV.96). At last the sails of Arthur's navy were seen.

Here one may look back to see how to this point my father had treated, and transformed, the narrative tradition that came to be known in later times in England from Malory's last tale, *The Death of Arthur.*

He preserved the 'chronicle' tradition of Arthur's eastern campaign overseas, but totally changed its nature and purpose. Arthur defends 'Rome', he does not assault it.

He retained the treason and usurpation of Mordred and his desire for Guinevere, but in a greatly developed portrait.

He introduced (*in a retrospect*) the 'romance' legend of Lancelot and Guinevere (entirely unknown to the 'chronicle' tradition), but greatly simplified the complex motives, deriving from the French *Mort Artu*, and found in the English stanzaic *Morte Arthur* and in Malory's last tale, by excising Gawain's part. He preserved the sentence of burning passed on Guinevere and her rescue by Lancelot; but his banishment now arose as punishment for his relationship with the queen, and not from Gawain's hatred of him for his slaying of Gareth. Lancelot is banished to Benwick, but Guinevere is restored to Arthur's favour.

The attack on Benwick by Arthur and Gawain was entirely excised, and the news of Mordred's treason reached Arthur not at Benwick but in the distant east.

*

Malory's Tale of the Death of Arthur (ii)

I will now sketch the concluding narrative of Malory's last tale, taking it up from where I left it (p.104) with Arthur's ships approaching Dover and Mordred awaiting him. Malory was now quite largely drawing on the English poem, the stanzaic *Morte Arthur,* for the detail of the narrative.

Arthur's host fought their way up from the beaches and with much bloodshed routed Mordred's people. But Sir Gawain was found, lying in a boat, 'more than halff dede'; and speaking to King Arthur he declared that through his pride and stubbornness he had caused his own death, for now he had been smitten in the place of the old wound that Lancelot gave him at Benwick; and that it was through him that Arthur suffered this grievous misfortune:

> for had that noble knyght, Sir Launcelot, ben with you, as he was and wolde have ben, thys unhappy warre had never ben begunne ..... And now ye shall mysse sir Launcelot. But alas that I wolde nat acccorde with hym!

And before he died he called for paper and pen to write a letter to Lancelot beseeching him to return in haste to aid King Arthur against Mordred.

Gawain was buried in the chapel in Dover Castle. But Mordred retreated to Barham Down in Kent, a few miles from Canterbury, and there Arthur came upon him: this battle ended with Mordred's flight to Canterbury. Arthur then withdrew westward to Salisbury Plain, and the two hosts prepared for a further encounter. But Sir Gawain appeared to Arthur in a dream, saying that he had been sent by God to warn him against further fighting until a month had passed, by which time Sir Lancelot would come from France with all his knights. A treaty was then negotiated with Mordred to this end, but broken by a mistaken fear of treachery; and there followed the third and most savage battle lasting all day till nightfall, and ending with King Arthur and Sir Bedivere and Sir Lucan on the one hand, and Mordred on the other, standing amid vast numbers of slain men. But the king caught sight of Mordred 'leanyng uppon his swerde amonge a grete hepe of dede men'; and racing towards each other Arthur ran Mordred through with his spear. Then Mordred knew that he had got his death wound, but with his last strength 'he smote hys fadir, kynge Arthure, with hys swerde holdynge in both hys hondys, uppon the syde of the hede, that the swerde perced the helmet', and with that Mordred 'daysshed downe starke dede to the erthe'.

Then Sir Bedivere and Sir Lucan, themselves severely wounded, carried the king to 'a lytyll chapell nat farre from the see'. Hearing a great clamour from the battlefield, for robbers had come to pillage the slain, the two knights thought it best to carry the king further off, but as they did so Sir Lucan fell dead from his wounds. Then Arthur ordered Bedivere to take his sword Excalibur, to cast it into 'yondir watirs syde', and returning tell him what he had seen. Twice Bedivere went to the water, and each time he feigned that he had done what he was bidden; but each time King Arthur told him in anger that he lied. For a third time Bedivere went 'unto the watirs syde', and returning told truthfully that he had hurled the sword as far as he could, whereupon an arm had risen from the water, caught the sword and brandished it, and then drew it down and disappeared.

Then, as the king commanded, Bedivere carried him on his back to the water's edge, where 'faste by the banke hoved [*waited*] a lytyll barge with many fayre ladyes in hit, and amonge them all was a quene', she being Arthur's sister, Morgan la Fée. Then Bedivere laid Arthur in the barge, and Morgan said (following the words in the stanzaic *Morte Arthur*) 'A, my dere brother! Why have ye taryed so longe from me? Alas, thys wounde on youre hede hath caught over-much coulde!' But as the barge departed Bedivere cried out to the king asking what should become of him; and he answered:

Comforte thyselff, and do as well as thou mayste, for in me ys no truste for to truste in. For I muste into the vale of Avylyon to hele me of my grevous wounde. And if thou here nevermore of me, pray for my soule!

Next day, in his wandering Bedivere came upon 'a chapell and an ermytage' where there was a newly dug grave, concerning which the hermit told him that 'a number of ladies' had come at midnight and brought the body to him for burial (on this matter see p.142). Then Bedivere remained at the hermitage, which was 'besydes Glassyngbyry' (Glastonbury in Somerset), and lived with the hermit 'in prayers and fastynges and grete abstynaunce'. But when Guinevere learned of all that had happened she 'stole away' and came to Amysbyry (Amesbury in Wiltshire), and there became a nun:

> and never creature coude make her myry, but ever she lyved in fastynge, prayers, and almes-dedis, that all manèr of people mervayled how vertuously she was chaunged.

When Lancelot in Benwick learned of what had come to pass in England, and had received Gawain's letter, in great haste he made ready a host and crossed the sea to Dover. There he found that he was too late. He visited in great grief the tomb of Gawain in the chapel of Dover Castle, and then he rode away westwards until he came to the convent where Guinevere had become a nun. When she saw him again she fell into a swoon, but recovering she said to the assembled nuns, in the presence of Lancelot:

> Thorow thys same man and me hath all thys warre be wrought, and the deth of the moste nobelest knyghtes of the worlde; for thorow oure love that we have loved togydir ys my moste noble lorde slayne. Therefore, sir Launcelot, wyte thou well I am sette in suche a plyght to get my soule hele [*healing, health*].

In the words between them, which cannot be shortened or sketched, she remained adamant, refusing him when he said 'I praye you kysse me, and never no more.' And so they parted, 'but there was never so harde an herted man but he wold have wepte to see the dolour that they made, for there was lamentacyon as they had be stungyn with sperys.'

After Lancelot left Amesbury he came upon the hermitage where Bedivere now lived, and he stayed there, and led the same manner of life. Other knights of the Round Table came to join them there; and after six years Lancelot became a priest. One night he had a vision, in which he was told that he must go to to Amesbury, where he would find Guinevere dead, and that she must be buried by the side of King Arthur. With his companions Lancelot went on foot 'from Glastynburye to Almysburye, the whiche is lytel more than thirty myle', but they took two days, for they were weak and feeble from their lives of penance and fasting. When they reached Amesbury they learned that Guinevere had died only half an hour before; and they were told that she had said of Lancelot that

'hyder he cometh as faste as he may to fetche my cors, and besyde my lord kyng Arthur he shal berye me.' Wherefore the quene sayd in heryng of them al, 'I beseche Almyghty God that I may never have power to see syr Launcelot wyth my worldly eyen!'

And so Guinevere was carried back to the chapel near Glastonbury, and there she was buried.

Thereafter Lancelot would eat and drink so little that 'he dryed and dwyned awaye', and before long he died. After a journey of fifteen days his body was brought according to his wish to the castle of Joyous Garde, and was buried in the choir of the chapel there.

*

The alliterative Morte Arthure (ii)

From the moment when the sails of Arthur's fleet were seen from the coast my father turned away from the tradition embodied in English in the stanzaic *Morte Arthur* and Malory's *Tale of the Death of Arthur* and turned to the alliterative *Morte Arthur*, whose narrative I left at the point where Arthur learned from Sir Cradoc of Mordred's treachery and his wedding to Guinevere (p.84).

In the stanzaic *Morte Arthur* and in Malory there was no confrontation at sea to Arthur on his return, but in the alliterative poem it was a part of Sir Cradoc's ill news that Mordred had raised a fleet against him (p.84):

Att Southamptone on the see   es seuene skore [s]chippes,
frawghte fulle of ferse folke,   owt of ferre landes.

The author conveys in a few lines the speed of the return of Arthur, who

Turnys thorowe Tuskayne,   taries bot littill,
Lyghte noghte in Lumbarddye   bot when the lyghte failede;
Merkes ouer the mowntaynes   full mervaylous wayes ...

'and within fyftene dayes his flete es assemblede' (in *The Fall of Arthur*, II.76–88, Radbod gives to Mordred a vivid account of Arthur's preparations).

But now in the alliterative *Morte Arthure* the poet devoted some hundred lines to the evocation of a violent sea-battle that followed, to which there is nothing comparable in mediaeval English literature. There is a furious onset of words, conveying (one might say, as much by their form and conjunctions as by their meaning) the roar of the battle, the splitting of timbers, ships crashing together, trumpets blowing, arrows flying, masts falling ...

It was from this poem that my father derived his portrayal of a great sea-battle off the coast of Kent on Arthur's return. In earlier works of the 'chronicle' tradition there was fierce fighting when Arthur's fleet came in, but it was a battle between invaders from the sea opposed by Mordred's host defending the cliffs. In Laȝamon's *Brut* (see pp.78, 146) this is made very plain, and that my father had the passage in mind when he wrote of the sea-battle is seen from the words in the *Brut* telling that Arthur 'hehte [ordered] þat his scip-men brohten hine to Romerel', whence he took the name Romeril (Romney in Kent, already referred to, p.110).

In the sea-battle in *The Fall of Arthur* there are echoes no doubt of the alliterative *Morte Arthure* in such lines as (IV.180–2)

Beak met bulwark.   Burst were timbers.
There was clang of iron   and crash of axes;
sparked and splintered   spears and helmets ...

but there is no trace, naturally enough, of the triumphant, exultant tone of the old poem, where 'our' lords are seen laughing loudly at the foreigners in Mordred's fleet who leap in terror into the sea ('when ledys [men] of owtlonndys leppyn in waters, / All oure lordes one lowde laughen at ones').

It is convenient here to give an account, in some parts more condensed than in others, of the conclusion of the alliterative *Morte Arthure*.

The battle of the ships was won, but 'Yitt es the traytoure one londe with tryede knyghttes', awaiting the attempt by the incomers to force a landing against them; and from this the king was prevented, for the tide had by now gone out, leaving great slushy pools. But Gawain took a galley [a large open boat] and with a small band of men came ashore, sinking to his waist in his golden garments ('to the girdylle he gos in alle his gylte wedys') and then racing across the sands, where they hurled thselves against the host of Mordred arrayed before them. Gawain struck down the King of Gothland, and then crying 'Fy on the, felone, and thy false werkys!' made for Mordred 'among all his men, with the Montagues and other great lords'; but he and his band were surrounded and hopelessly outnumbered ('We are beset by Saracens on all sides!').

Gawain fell then into a crazed recklessness, as the poet repeatedly declares: 'all his witte faylede'; 'alls unwyse, wodewyse' [as one reckless and mad]; 'he fell in a fransye for fersenesse of herte'; 'wode [mad] alls a wylde beste'. Finally in a hand-to-hand encounter with Mordred he was worsted, and fell dead from a blow that pierced his helmet. Mordred was questioned by King Frederic of Friesland, who saw Gawain's deeds:

> Qwat gome was he this   with the gaye armes
> With this gryffoune of golde,   that es one growffe fallyn?*

And Mordred named him, and greatly praised him:

> Had thow knawen hym, sir kynge,   'in kythe thare he lengede,
> His konynge, his knyghthode,   his kyndly werkes,
> His doyng, his doughtyness,   his dedis of armes,
> Thow wolde hafe dole for his dede   the dayes of thy lyfe!'
>   Yit that traytour alls tite   teris lete he falle,
> Turnes hym furthe tite,   and talkes no more,
> Went wepand awaye,   and weries the stowndys,
> That ever his werdes ware wroght,   siche wandrethe to wyrke.†

'Repenting of all his grievous deeds' he went away westwards, to Cornwall, and pitched his tents by the river named Tambire (Tamar). From there he sent a messenger to Guinevere at York,

---

* *Qwat gome* What man; *one growffe* on his face.

† *in kythe thare he lengede* in the land where he lived; *konynge* skill; *dole for his dede* sorrow for his death; *tite* quickly; *furthe* forth; *weries the stowndys* curses the time[s]; *werdes* fates; *wandrethe* woe.

telling her of all that had taken place, and bidding her flee 'with her children' to Ireland; but she leaving York in the deepest despondency went to Caerleon, and there took the veil:

> Askes thare the habite in the honoure of Criste,
> and all for falsede, and frawde, and fere of hire loverde [lord]!

But Arthur seeing the madness of Gawain rushed from his ship with many knights, and searching the battlefield found his body 'in his gaye armes, umbegrippede the girse, and on grouffe fallen' (clutching the grass, fallen on his face). In an extremity of grief he uttered a passionate lament for Gawain (on this see pp.129–31), whose body was taken to a monastery at Winchester. The king was advised to stay a while in Winchester to assemble his forces before pursuing Mordred, but Arthur would have none of it, expressing his hatred of Mordred in violent words, and vowing to 'ever pursue the payganys that my pople distroyede'. He departed at once from Winchester and went west to Cornwall, where he came upon Mordred encamped in a forest. Challenged to battle, Mordred's huge host, vastly outnumbering that of the king, emerged from the forest.

Then follows the battle of Camlan (but it is not named in the poem), a ferocious fight to the death of 'the bolde Bretons' [i.e. Britons] against such foes as 'Peghttes and paynymes [Picts and pagans] with perilous wapyns' and 'ethyns [giants] of Argyle and Irische kynges', told in some two hundred lines, with many individual encounters; many knights who fell are named, among them Marrac, Meneduc and Errac (who are named in *The Fall of Arthur*, I.48–9) – and Lancelot (on his presence and death at Camlan see pp.91–3). The battle ends with the fight to the death of Mordred and Arthur, with a graphic description of each hideous sword-thrust. Though he had received his death-wound, Arthur wielding his sword Caliburn slashed off the sword-hand of Mordred and ran him through as he lay on the grass.

But the king still lived.

> Thane they holde at his heste   hally at ones
> And graythes to Glasschenberye   the gate at the gayneste;
> Entres the Ile of Aveloyne,   and Arthure he lyghttes,
> Merkes to a manere there,   for myghte he no forthire.*

A surgeon of Salerno examined his wounds, and Arthur saw that he would never be healed. On his death-bed he ordered that Mordred's children should be killed and drowned ('Latt no wykkyde wede waxe, ne wrythe [*flourish*] one this erthe'), and his last words were of Guinevere:

> I foregyffe all greffe,   for Cristez lufe of hevene!
> Yife Waynor hafe wele wroghte,   wele hir betydde!

King Arthur was buried at Glastonbury, and with his burial the alliterative *Morte Arthure* ends.

---

* *heste* command; *hally* wholly; *graythes to Glasschenberye* make their way to Glastonbury; *the gate at the gayneste* by the shortest road; *merkes to a manere* goes to a manor-house.

Thus endis kyng Arthure,   as auctors alegges,
That was of Ectores blude,   the kynge sone of Troye,
And of Pyramous, the prynce,   praysede in erthe;
Fro thethen broghte the Bretons   alle his bolde eldyrs
Into Bretayne the brode,   as the Bruytte tellys.*

At the victorious end of the sea-battle, with Arthur on his ship off Romeril, gazing at his own land in doubt of his best course, my father ceased to work on *The Fall of Arthur*: in my view, one of the most grievous of his many abandonments.

*

---

* *thethen* thence; *Bretons* Britons; *eldyrs* ancestors; *Bruytte* Brut (see p.78, footnote).

THE UNWRITTEN POEM
AND ITS RELATION TO
THE SILMARILLION

THE UNWRITTEN POEM
AND ITS RELATION TO
THE SILMARILLION

The abandonment of *The Fall of Arthur* is qualified by the existence of manuscript notes of various value that indicate my father's thoughts and intentions for the continuation and con- clusion of the poem, and of some of these it must be said that their content is both extremely interesting and extremely tan- talizing. There are also scraps of further verse, though almost all are written so rapidly as to be in places beyond certain interpretation. Among these papers is a sketch of the narrative to follow the last part of the finished text, where Arthur, pon- dering the nature and outcome of an assault on the cliffs, opens his thought to Gawain that they would best postpone further conflict, and 'trusting to the wind and the ebb-tide' sail west along the coast 'to other landing' (V.61–3).

I give here this sketch: clearly contemporary with the con- cluding passage of the poem, it takes up no more than a single page, written in a manner somewhat but not greatly above my father's most impenetrable. I have expanded contractions and introduced trivial corrections for clarity.

Counsel. Arthur does not wish to risk his knights. He calls Gawain and proposes to turn west and run with wind and ebb down the channel west to other landing – ere Mordred could follow in power, to Cornwall of unkindly coast by kind people or to fair Lyonesse.*

But Gawain says we planned to attack Mordred right away. There he is. Sooner or later we must attack him. Every day adds to his strength and leaves the East open to the [? heathen].†

They gaze till the sun sinks. Gawain gazed in fretted wrath.

---

* On other pages my father scribbled down alliterative lines and half-lines that follow from this summary, and this last sentence would be scarcely more than guesswork were it not confirmed by these lines on another page:

> To Cornwall coming
> of coast unkind but kind people
> or in Lyonesse find loyal welcome.

Lyonesse is the name of the lost land west of the most westerly point of Cornwall ('Land's End'). In my father's early tale of Ælfwine of England (see pp.152–3) is found the following (*The Book of Lost Tales Part II*, p.313):

> Though Déor [father of Ælfwine] was of English blood, it is told that he wedded to wife a maiden from the West, from Lionesse as some have named it since, or Evadrien 'Coast of Iron' as the Elves still say. Déor found her in the lost land beyond Belerion whence the Elves at times set sail.

† Scraps of verse on other pages, beginning 'Gawain answered in grave wonder', show my father's first movements towards the versification of this passage in the outline, in which he reminds Arthur of their firm resolve and settled purpose.

[*Written in the margin*: Arthur insists on leaving.] As the suns westers the tide turns again. Gawain leaps into a light boat with his dearest friends, and bidding all that dare follow him they drive their craft with oars and ground it on the white beaches. Gawain leaps overboard and under a hail of arrows wades ashore and up the river course, seeking to win a passage to the cliff tops. Mordred eggs on his men. That day Gawain missed Gaheris and Gareth and dour-handed Agravain his brethren.*

But he slew many men, ... level with those that stood on higher ground. He reaches the top but few are with him, though many are following. There he clears a way to Mordred. They fight and Gawain [?? falters]. The sun is sinking on his left hand [*written above:* lights his shield]. A red ray strikes on his shield and lights up the griffon [*on the shield*]. Galuth [*Gawain's sword*] breaks Mordred's helm and he falls back among his men, but snatches [a bow] from Ivor and turning shoots Gawain through the breast. Gawain falls, calling upon Arthur. Geryn, Gawain's

---

* On another page are found these lines written with more care (see p.96):

          in his wake followed
    lieges of Lothian. But Lot's children
    Gaheris and Gareth Gawain's brethren
    that day missed he, and dour-handed
    Sir Agravain: under earth lay they
    by Lancelot in luckless hour
    slain   to his long sorrow

esquire, slays Ivor, and Gawain's household fall on so fiercely that they win the cliff-top and stand about his body until Arthur's host comes [?? pressing] up. Arthur comes as Gawain dies, and the sun sinks beyond Lyonesse.

Here this outline ends. Another, evidently somewhat earlier, projects the narrative for the whole of the rest of the poem from the beginning of the fourth canto; but from Arthur's lament for Gawain it is reduced (if written at the same time as the outline, which is not certain) to hasty notes on two sides of a single page, and there are no other clues to my father's thoughts for the remainder of the poem.

Bright sun shines over Britain. Mordred's men are beating the woods for Guinevere, and they cannot find her. In the meanwhile sending men to the land of Leodogrance (Camiliard in Wales) he goes east and assembles his host joining with the Saxons and Frisians. Wind blew fair from the south and the sea lay green beneath the white cliffs. Mordred had beacons built on cliff tops and hills, so that his host might assemble to whatever point Arthur came.

The ships of Arthur are seen approaching. A white lady with a child in her arms is Arthur's ensign. Before Arthur's ship sails a great white ship with a banner of a golden griffin. The sun is embroidered on its sails. That is Gawain. Still Mordred hesitates and will not have fire set in the beacon. For he thought in his heart, if Lancelot and Ban's kindred were in the navy he would draw off and make peace. For if he hated Lancelot the more he was of him now afraid. But the white lily on the black field of Lancelot was not seen, for Lancelot awaited the Queen's summons. Then at last the beacon flamed and Mordred's host held the shore. Thus Arthur came to Romeril.

The Saxon ships before Romeril were driven away or sunk and set on fire, but Arthur could not land and was held back. So Gawain thrust forth his ship Wingelot (?)* and others of his vassals, and they ground upon the white beach, which is soon stained red. The battle is fierce. Gawain leaps overboard and wades ashore. His yellow hair is seen towering above his dark foes. He slays the King of Gothland, and hews his way to Mordred's standard. Duel of Gawain and Mordred. Mordred driven back, but he catches a bow from a henchman and turns and shoots Gawain. [*Written in margin:* Mordred saved by Ivor.]

Gawain falls and dies by the rim of Ocean, calling for Arthur. In the meanwhile the fury of Gawain's men clears the shore and Arthur comes and kisses Gawain farewell.

Arthur's lament.

I give here, for a reason that will quickly be apparent, both King Arthur's lament from the alliterative *Morte Arthure* and its form in *The Fall of Arthur*.

Than gliftis the gud kynge,   and glopyns in herte,
Gronys ful grisely   with gretande teris;

---

* The question mark following 'Wingelot' is not editorial. On this name see pp.158, 160.

Knelis downe to the cors, and kaught it in armes,
Kastys upe his umbrere, and kyssis hym sone,
Lookes one his eye-liddis, that lowkkide ware faire,
His lipis like to the lede, and his lire falowede.
Than the corownde kyng cryes fulle lowde:
'Dere kosyn o kynde, in kare am I levede,
For nowe my wirchipe es wente and my were endide.
Here es the hope of my hele, my happynge of armes,
My herte and my hardynes hale on hym lengede,
My concelle, my comforthe, that kepide myne herte!
Of alle knyghtes the kynge that undir Criste lifede,
Thou was worthy to be kynge, thofe I the corown bare.
My wele and my wirchipe of all this werlde riche
Was wonnen thourghe sir Gawayne, and thourghe his witt
    one!
Allas!' saide sir Arthure, 'nowe ekys my sorowe!
I am uttirly undon in my awen landes!
A! dowttouse derfe dede, thou duellis to longe!
Why drawes thou so one dreghe? thow drownnes myn
    herte!'*

---

* *gliftis* looks; *glopyns* is distressed, is confounded; *grisely* terribly;
gretande weeping; *umbrere* visor; *lowkkide* closed; *lede* lead; *lire*
face; *falowede* grown pale; *o kynde* by kin; *levede* left; *wirchipe*
honour; *were* war; *hele* well-being, prosperity; *happynge* good
fortune; *hale* wholly; *kepide* guarded, protected; *thofe* though; *one*
alone; *ekys* is increased; *dowttouse derfe dede* dread, stern death;
duellis tarry; *drawes ... one dreghe* draw ... aside, hold back.

The lamentation of King Arthur for Sir Gawain in *The Fall of Arthur* papers is at once in the very earliest stage of composition and unhappily in my father's most inscrutable hand. After much study this is the best rendering that I have been able to produce.

Then gloom fell grey   on the good king's heart
and he groans   amid gliding tears
looking upon his eyes   now closed for ever
and his lips like lead   and [? lily faded].
Then his [? crown] he cast down   crying aloud
   'Dear kinsman   in care am I left
now my glory is gone   and my grace [*written above:* good]
   ended.
Here lies my hope and my help   and my helm and my sword
my heart and my hardihood   and my ..... of strength
my counsel and comfort
of all knights the [?? noblest].
of all [?kings] the .... Christ lived
To be king .... I the crown bore.
I am ...... [?utterly ruined]   in mine own lands.
Ah, dread death   thou dwellest too long,
thou drownest my heart   ere I die.

In the *Alliterative Morte Arthure* the king is reproved by his knights for his indecorous display of grief:

'Blyne', sais thies bolde men,   'thow blondirs thi selfen;
This es botles bale,   for bettir bees it never.

It es no wirchipe iwysse   to wryng thyn hondes;
To wepe als a woman,   it es no witt holden.
Be knyghtly of contenaunce,   als a kyng scholde,
And leve siche clamoure   for Cristes lufe of heven!'*

My father dashed down a few words here, with a heading 'Sir Iwain comforts him with Beowulf's words':

> to weep as a woman is not wit holden
> better vengeance than lament

The passage from *Beowulf* in my father's mind is I think certainly Beowulf's words to Hrothgar, King of the Danes, in lines 1384–9 of the poem:

> Ne sorge, snotor guma!   Selre bið æghwæm,
> þæt his freond wrece,   þonne he fela murne.
> Ure æghwylc sceal   ende gebidan
> worold lifes,   wyrce se þe mote
> domes ær deaþe;   þæt bið drihtguman
> unlifgendum   æfter selest.

> Grieve not, wise one! Better is it for every man
> that he should avenge his friend than he should much
> lament.

---

* *Blyne* cease; *blondirs* distract; *botles* without cure; *bale* grief; *bees* will be.

To each one of us shall come the end of life in the world;
let him who may earn glory ere his death. No better thing
can brave knight leave behind when he lies dead.

In the *Alliterative Morte Arthure* there follows a vow made by
King Arthur:

'Here I make myn avowe,' quod the kynge than,
'To Messie and to Marie,   the mylde qwenne of heven,
I sall never ryvaye   ne racches uncowpyll
At roo ne rayne-dere,   that rynnes appone erthe;
Never grewhownde late glyde,   ne gossehawke latt flye,
Ne never fowle see fellide,   that flieghes with wenge;
Fawkon ne formaylle   appon fiste handill,
Ne yitt with gerefawcon   rejoyse me in erthe;
Ne regnne in my royaltez,   ne halde my Rownde Table,
Till thi dede, my dere,   be dewly revengede;
Bot eveer droupe and dare,   qwylls my lyfe lastez,
Till Drighten and derfe dede   hafe don qwate them likes!'*

My father's initial thought for a rendering of the king's vow to
deny himself all forms of his principal pleasure reads thus:

Arthur's vow
I will never hunt with hounds nor with hawk

---

* *Messie* Messiah; *ryvaye* hunt by a river; *racches* hounds; *roo ne rayene-dere* roe deer nor reindeer; *fellide* felled; *formaylle* female hawk; *dede* death; *dare* lie still; *Drighten* the Lord; *derfe* hard, stern.

Nor feast nor hear harp nor bear crown
[? nor sit at] the Round Table till I have avenged Gawain.

It needs no discussion to see that if my father did not have the *Alliterative Morte Arthure* open in front of him, at the very least he had read this passage very recently, when he sketched out an initial version of Arthur's lament for Gawain and his vow of self-denial.

I have already observed (p.117) that the conception of a great sea-battle off Romeril in *The Fall of Arthur* was derived from the alliterative poem. From the outlines given above other features of this nature can be added. From the *Morte Arthure* come the ebbing of the tide, hindering Arthur from landing (pp.118, 129), and Gawain's taking a boat with a few companions and then wading ashore (pp.118, 127). Gawain's slaying of the King of Gothland in the fighting on land is from the same source (pp.118, 129) – but in the finished poem this is placed earlier, in the course of the sea-battle (IV.202–3). Among other details are the name of Gawain's sword, *Galuth* (IV.197–200), and the golden griffon on his ship's banner (IV.144) and his shield (pp.119, 127).

It remains now to return to the second of the two outlines and the tantalizing notes that follow Arthur's lament for Gawain, which are all that exist to give any idea of how my father saw the conclusion of *The Fall of Arthur* at about the time when he abandoned it.

Beneath the drafting for Arthur's lament and vow is written:

Mordred is driven off and retires east. Arthur goes west. Lancelot ... [?? the body of Gawain]. *In the margin is written, presumably referring to Mordred:* for lack of support all the east is held by him. *At the foot of the page is jotted in pencil:* Begin Canto V with Gawain's body being borne to Camelot.

On another page are the following notes, written very rapidly indeed: in my transcript several words are scarcely more than guesses.

Strong sun. Arms of Arthur move first. Rumour of Mordred's attack. A little cloud in the East. Mordred comes unexpectedly out of a forest upon the Plain of Camlan. Iwain and Errak. Marrac and Meneduc. Idris and Ailmer.

Mordred has Saxons Frisians Irish Picts and Paynims [*i.e. Pagans*] with perilous weapons (see p.120). Arthur borne back. Mordred issues last. Arthur and Mordred slay one other. The cloud [?gathers] to darkness. All grows dark.

Arthur retires into the west. Rumour of Mordred's advance. Mordred issues from forest.
Battle of Camlan. Arthur and Mordred slay one another. Cloud [?gathers]. Arthur dying in the gloom. Robbers search the field.

[Excalibur >] Caliburn and the lake. The dark ship comes up the river. Arthur placed upon it.

Lancelot has no news. On a grey day of [?? rain] he sets sail with Lionel and comes to Romeril where the crows are still over Romeril. As he rides along the empty roads the Queen comes down out of Wales and meets him. But he only asks where is Arthur. She does not know.

He turns from her and rides ever west. The hermit by the sea shore tells him of Arthur's departure. Lancelot gets a boat and sails west and never returns. – Eärendel passage.

Guinevere watching afar sees his silver banner vanish under the moon. Thus she came utterly to grief. She fled to Wales from the men of the east, but though grief was her lot it is not said that she mourned more for others than for herself. But so ended the glory of Arthur and the prowess of the ancient world, and there was a long darkness over the land of Britain.

Other hastily pencilled notes tell a little more of Lancelot and Guinevere.

Lancelot came too late hearing of Camlan, and meets Guinevere, but his lord loving all his love went to him. His love for Guinevere had no more power. In [?? pain] they parted cold and griefless. [?? She is alone.]

Lancelot parts from Guinevere and sets sail for Benwick but turns west and follows after Arthur. And never returns from the sea. Whether he found him in Avalon and will return no one knows.

> Guinevere grew grey in the grey shadow
> all things losing who at all things grasped.
> ..... gold .... and was laid in dust
> as profitless to men as it proved of old.

With these papers are found on a separate sheet seventeen lines of alliterative verse in typescript, and from this fact and from the mention of Avalon in line 15 it is obvious that this is the 'Eärendel passage' referred to in the second outline above.

> The moon mounted the mists of the sea,
> and quivering in the cold the keen starlight
> that wavered wan in the waiting East
> failed and faded; the foam upon the shore
> was glimmering ghostly on the grey shingle,
> and the roaring of the sea rose in darkness
> to the watchers on the wall.
>   O! wondrous night
> when shining like the moon, with shrouds of pearl,
> with sails of samite, and the silver stars
> on her blue banner embroidered white
> in glittering gems, that galleon was thrust
> on the shadowy seas under shades of night!
> Eärendel goeth on eager quest

to magic islands beyond the miles of the sea,
past the hills of Avalon and the halls of the moon,
the dragon's portals and the dark mountains
of the Bay of Faery on the borders of the world.

The first seven lines were later hastily altered by my father thus, largely for metrical improvement.

The moon was fallen into misty caves,
and quivering cold the keen starlight
wavered wanly in the waiting East
failed and faded; the foam upon the shore
was glimmering ghostly upon grey shingle,
and the roaring sea rising and falling
under walls of stone.

On another page is a pencilled text of verses in the primary stage of composition, with deletions and substitutions, of exceptional difficulty, but of the utmost interest in relation to the 'Eärendel pasage' just given.

The grave of Gawain   under grass lieth
by the sounding sea,   where the sun westers.
What grave hath Guinever   The grey shadow
her gold in [?ground]   [(*struck out:*) gleams like]
her gold in silence   unseen gleameth.
Britain nor Benwick   did barrow keep
of Lancelot   and his lady.
No [(*struck out:*)   grave hath Arthur]

No mound hath Arthur   in mortal land
under moon or sun   who in ....
beyond the miles of the sea   and the magic islands
beyond the halls of night   upon Heaven's borders
[(*struck out:*) the] dragon's portals   and the dark mountains
of the Bay of Avalon   on the borders of the world.
up[on] Earth's border   in Avalon [sleeping >] biding.
While the world w....eth
till the world [??awaketh]

In the penultimate line the verb is not *waiteth* and seems not to
be *watcheth*. Beneath the verses is written: The tomb

*

The departure of Arthur

Among the scanty and enigmatic notes that I have given on
pp.135–7 there is so little that refers to the departure of Arthur
after his mortal wounding in the battle of Camlan that must
one look to other writings in the attempt to interpret them.

   Of the departure of Arthur we have only these sentences
(pp.135–6): *Arthur dying in the gloom. Robbers search the
field. Caliburn and the lake. The dark ship comes up the river.
Arthur placed in it.* And subsequently we read that Lancelot
sailed into the west following Arthur, but never returns,
and *Whether he found him in Avalon and will return no one
knows.*

I have given on p.113 Malory's account of Arthur's departure. In this he was following the stanzaic *Morte Arthur* fairly closely, rather than the French *Mort Artu* (see p.93). The most curious point, in relation to my father's notes, concerns the place and nature of Arthur's departure. In *Le Morte Arthur* it is said of the king and the knights Bedivere and Lucan that 'all night they in the chapel lay by the sea side', and Malory has 'not far from the sea'. In *Le Morte Arthur* Arthur orders Bedivere to cast Excalibur 'in the *salt flood*', and when Bedivere finally obeys the command 'into the *sea* he cast it': here Malory used the word 'water' (p.113), but Bedivere reports to the king that he saw *wawes* (waves). In the *Mort Artu*, however, the water is specifically a lake, as in my father's note: *Caliburn and the lake*. In Malory the vessel in which Arthur departed was 'a lytyll barge', in *Le Morte Arthur* it was 'a riche shyppe with maste and ore'.

Thus, in his intention, never fulfilled, my father had abandoned the conclusion of the alliterative *Morte Arthur*, where it is told of Arthur's death (p.121) that after the battle of Camlan he was carried, as he desired, to Glastonbury and entered 'the Ile of Aveloyne', where he died. He was now following the story derived in essentials from the *Mort Artu*. But it is difficult to interpret the 'lake' in his notes; as is also the ship that 'comes up the river'.

It doesn't seem that the ancient evidences concerning the battle of Camlan shed any light on my father's conception here. The earliest record is found in a chronicle of the tenth century known as the *Annales Cambriae*, the Annals of Wales, which has an entry under the year 537 *Gueith*

Camlann (the Battle of Camlan) 'in which Arthur and Medraut fell.' Geoffrey of Monmouth said that the battle took place in Cornwall, on the river *Cambula*, but gave no other indication. In fact, it is not known where Camlan of the *Annales Cambriae* was, not even whether it was in Cornwall; but it came to be identified with the Cornish river Camel.[*]

The river that bore Arthur away in my father's note must derive ultimately from Geoffrey of Monmouth's *Cambula*. But the apparent incongruities in these notes are best explained, I think, on the supposition that they represent his ideas in an unformed state: glimpses of scenes which were not as yet coherent and unified: the chapel by the sea, Excalibur cast into the sea – or lake, the river which brings the mysterious ship on which Arthur departs.

It is in any case abundantly clear that he would have nothing to do with the ending of the story of Arthur himself in the *Mort Artu,* in the stanzaic *Morte Arthur*, and in Malory (see pp. 113–4): the burial of his body at the hermitage to which it had been brought on the night following his departure in the ship – in the words of the hermit to Bedivere in *Le Morte Arthur*,

> Abowte mydnyght were ladyes here,
> In world ne wyste I what they were,
> This body they brought uppon a bere
> And beryed it wyth woundys sore.

---

[*] This river, of no great length, rises near Camelford (west of Launceston) and flows into the sea near Padstow (north-west of Bodmin).

But Malory's actual words about the burial of Arthur at the hermitage chapel near Glastonbury are curious.

'Sir,' seyde sir Bedyvere, 'what man ys there here entyred that ye pray so faste fore?'

'Fayre sunne,' seyde the ermyte, 'I wote nat veryly but by demynge [*guessing*]. But thys same nyght, at mydnyght, here cam a numbir of ladyes and brought here a dede corse and prayde me to entyre [*bury*] him. And here they offird an hondred tapers, and they gaff me a thousande besauntes.'

'Alas!' seyde sir Bedyvere, 'that was my lorde kynge Arthur, which lyethe here gravyn [*buried*] in thys chapell.'

Thus of Arthur I fynde no more wrytten in bokis that bene auctorysed, nothir more of this verray sertaynté of hys deth harde I never rede, but thus was he lad away in a shyp wherein were three quenys .....

Now more of the deth of kynge Arthur coude I never fynde, but that thes ladyes brought hym to hys grave ..... But yet the ermyte knew nat in sertayne that he was veryly the body of kynge Arthur; for thys tale sir Bedwere, a knyght of the Table Rounde, made hit to be wrytten.

It seems plain that Malory was very sceptical of the strange story that he found in his sources.

But in respect of Arthur's destination in the barge, or ship, his last words to Bedivere in Malory's tale, already cited on p.113, must be recalled: 'For I muste into the vale of Avylyon to hele me of my grevous wounde. And if thou here nevermore of me, pray for my soule!' Malory was echoing Arthur's words in *Le Morte Arthur*, here in response to the cry of Bedivere 'lord, whedyr are ye bowne?' [*Whither are you bound*?]:

I wylle wende a lytelle stownde [*while*]
In to the vale of Aveloune,
A whyle to hele me of my wounde.

This reference to the vale of Avalon is absent from the *Mort Artu*. In *The Fall of Arthur* it was of course to Avalon that the king was going. But where was Avalon?

In my father's poem it was emphatically not Glastonbury in Somerset. In the notes given on p.136 Sir Lancelot, returned to Britain from Benwick, rides westward; and '*the hermit by the sea shore tells him of Arthur's departure.*' Then 'Lancelot gets a boat and sails west and never returns.' It seems to me all but certain that this hermit was the keeper of the chapel 'not far from the sea' or 'by the sea side' (p.140) to which Sir Lucan and Sir Bedivere brought the wounded king, though he is not mentioned in *Le Morte Arthur* or Malory. On this view, he saw, and told what he saw to Sir Lancelot, the ship bearing Arthur away from the coast, out to sea, and certainly not in the direction of a hermitage near Glastonbury for burial.

The association of Arthur's grave with Glastonbury can therefore be described briefly. The earliest written record is found in a work of the Welsh antiquary Giraldus Cambrensis, or Gerald of Wales, written near the end of the twelfth century. After observing that fantastical tales were told of Arthur's body, as that it had been borne to a region far away by spirits and was not subject to death, he said that 'in our days' Arthur's body had in fact been found, by the monks of the abbey of Glastonbury, buried deep in the ground in a hollowed oak in the graveyard. A leaden cross was fixed to the underside of a stone beneath the coffin, in such a way that an inscription on the cross was concealed. The inscription, which Giraldus had himself seen, declared that buried there was the renowned King Arthur together with Wennevaria *in insula Avallonia* [*in the island Avallonia*]. (He records also the curious detail that beside the bones of Arthur (which were of huge size) and of Guinevere was a perfectly preserved tress of her golden hair, but that when it was touched by one of the monks it fell instantly to dust.) The date of this event is recorded as 1191.

In the same passage Giraldus said that what was now called *Glastonia* was anciently called *Insula Avallonia*. This name, he explained, arose because the place was virtually an island, entirely surrounded by marshes, whence it was called *Britannice* (in the British [i.e. Celtic] language) *Inis Avallon*, meaning, he said, *insula pomifera* 'island of apples', *aval* being the British word for 'apple', for apple-trees were once abundant there. He adds also that *Morganis*, who was a noble lady, akin to King Arthur, and

144

ruler of that region, took him after the battle of Kemelen (Camlan) to the island which is now called Glastonia for the healing of his wounds.

*

There is no need to pursue further the 'Glastonbury connection' into the complex questions of what lay behind this very curious 'discovery' of King Arthur's grave, and whether there were associations between Glastonbury and the legends of Arthur before 1191. It will however be clear how it came about that the author of the alliterative *Morte Arthure* could say (p.121) that Arthur was taken to *Glasschenberye*, and yet *entered the Ile of Aveloyne,* and how the king could say to Bedivere, in the stanzaic *Morte Arthur* and in Malory, as he lay in the ship, that he will go to the vale of Avalon for the healing of his wound (p.143).

But in *The Fall of Arthur* my father had no concern with Glastonbury in his reshaping of the legend. For him, beyond question, Avalon was an island in the remote West; but concerning its nature, in the notes that are appended to the poem, we learn nothing. There is a single, and mystifying, reference to Avalon in the poem itself (I.204). This is in a speech by Gawain in which he reminds King Arthur of his uncounted might in chivalric arms, 'from the Forest's margin to the Isle of Avalon': which must mean that Avalon had become a part of Arthur's dominion in the western seas, unless it is no more than a sweeping rhetorical suggestion of the extent of his power in East and West.

Of Arthur's departure Geoffrey of Monmouth in his *Historia Regum,* as already noted (p.78), said no more than that for the healing of his wounds he was borne to the Isle of Avalon (*in insulam Avallonis*). But in another, later work of his, the *Vita Merlini,* a poem in Latin hexameters, he gave an account of Avalon and the coming there of King Arthur, as if in the words of the Welsh bard Taliesin. In this poem the isle is named (using the same etymology, *aval* 'apple', as did Giraldus) *Insula pomorum que fortuna vocatur,* 'the Island of Apples, which is called the Fortunate Isle': for in this blessed land all things are brought forth of themselves: there is no need of farmers to plough the fields, where corn and grapes appear without tending. 'Thither after the battle of Camlan (*post bellum Camblani*) we took the wounded Arthur, and there we were received with honour by Morgen, who laid the king on a golden bed in her own chamber and looked long at the wound, saying at last that he could be restored to health if he were to stay with her for a long time and submit to her cure. Rejoicing therefore we committed the king to her and returning gave our sails to the following winds.'

The earliest account in literature of Arthur's departure in the ship is found in the *Brut* of Laȝamon, on which see p.78. According to Laȝamon the place of the great battle was Camelford, and the armies came together 'upon the Tambre', the river Tamar, which is a long way from Camelford. I cite here Laȝamon's lines on King Arthur's words as he lay mortally wounded on the ground and the coming of the boat that carried him away.* It will be seen that the metre is the heir to the ancestral form seen in *Beowulf* (and indeed in *The Fall of Arthur*) but with longer lines, the half-lines linked now by rhyme or assonance rather than alliteration; while the vocabulary is almost wholly Old English.

> 'And ich wulle varen to Avalun   to vairest alre maidene,
> to Argante þere quene,   alven swiðe sceone,
> and heo scal mine wunden   makien alle isunde,
> al hal me makien   mid haleweiȝe drenchen.
> And seoðe ich cumen wulle   to mine kinerichen
> and wunien mid Brutten   mid muchelere wunne.'
> Æfne þan worden   þer com of se wenden
> þat wes an sceort bat liðen   sceoven mid uðen,
> and twa wimmen þer inne   wunderliche idihte,
> and heo nommen Arður anan,   and aneouste hine vereden,
> and softe hine adun leiden   and forð gunnen hine liðen.
> . . . .
> Bruttes ileveð ȝete þat he bon on live,
> and wunnien in Avalun   mid fairest alre alven,
> and lokieð evere Bruttes ȝete   whan Arður cumen liðe.

---

* I have cited this text from the manuscript Cotton Caligula A ix in Sir Francis Madden's edition in three volumes of 1847, which for more than a century was the only edition of Laȝamon's *Brut*. My father acquired a very fine copy of this rare and costly work in 1927.

'And I will go to Avalon, to the fairest of all maidens,
to Argante the queen*, an elf most fair,
and she shall make whole my wounds
make me all whole with healing draughts.
And afterwards I will come again to my kingdom
and dwell among the Britons with great joy.'
Even with the words there came from the sea
a short boat journeying, driven by the waves,
and therein two women marvellously arrayed,
and forthwith they took up Arthur, and bore him swiftly,
and laid him gently down, and departed.

. . . .

The Britons believe yet that he lives
and dwells in Avalon with the fairest of all elves,
and the Britons ever yet await when Arthur will return.

This passage is peculiar to Laȝamon: there is nothing corresponding to it in Wace's *Brut*.

✳

In the case of *The Fall of Arthur* there is a further aspect of 'Avalon' to be considered: the perplexing question of the relationship between the 'island of apples' or 'Fortunate Isle', the Avalon to which King Arthur was taken, that was briefly described by Geoffrey of Monmouth in the *Vita*

---

* The name *Argante* seems likely to have been a corruption of *Morgen* in Geoffrey of Monmouth's *Vita Merlini* (see p.146).

Merlini (p.146), and the Avalon of my father's own imagined world.

It was a long time before that name emerged for the island called Tol Eressëa, the Lonely Isle, in the furthest waters of Belegaer, the Great Sea of the West; and there is no occasion here to enter into an account of my father's strangely changing vision of the Lonely Isle in the earlier years of 'The Silmarillion'. On the other hand, it is relevant to try to discern his thinking on the matter during the time when he was working on The Fall of Arthur.

The only precise date to assist in this is 9 December 1934, when R.W. Chambers wrote to congratulate him on *'Arthur'*, then in progress (p.10); but this of course gives no indication of how near he was at that time to abandoning the poem.

Long afterwards, in a letter of 16 July 1964, he told how he and C.S. Lewis had agreed, at some time now unknown, each to write a story: Lewis's to be a tale of space-travel and my father's a tale of time-travel. Lewis's *Out of the Silent Planet* was finished by the autumn of 1937, and my father's *The Lost Road*, very far indeed from finished, was sent with other works in a fateful parcel to Allen and Unwin in November of that year. In September *The Hobbit* had been published; on 19 December 1937 he said in a letter 'I have written the first chapter of a new story about Hobbits'.

Many years later he described, in that letter of 1964, his intentions for *The Lost Road*.

I began an abortive book of time-travel of which the end was to be the presence of my hero in the drowning of *Atlantis*. This was to be called *Númenor*, the Land in the West. The thread was to be the occurrence time and again in human families (like Durin among the Dwarves) of a father and son called by names that could be interpreted as Bliss-friend and Elf-friend. ..... It started with a father-son affinity between Edwin and Elwin of the present, and was supposed to go back into legendary time by way of an Eädwine and Ælfwine of circa A.D.918, and Audoin and Alboin of Lombardic legend, and so to the traditions of the North Sea concerning the coming of corn and culture heroes, ancestors of kingly lines, in boats (and their departure in funeral ships). ..... In my tale we were to come at last to Amandil and Elendil leaders of the loyal party in Númenor, when it fell under the domination of Sauron.

There survives (printed in *The Lost Road and Other Writings*, 1987, p.12) the original sketch of his 'idea' for the concluding legend that my father dashed down at great speed. 'This remarkable text,' I wrote of it in that book, 'documents the beginning of the legend of Númenor, and the extension of "The Silmarillion" into a Second Age of the world. Here the idea of the World Made Round and the Straight Path was first set down ...' There exist also two versions (*ibid.* pp.13 ff.), close in time, the second a revision of the first, of a brief narrative that was the forerunner of the *Akallabêth* (published with *The Silmarillion*). On the second text (only) my father later pencilled on the manuscript a title: *The Last Tale: The Fall of Númenor.*

My study of these texts showed that *The Fall of Númenor* and passages in *The Lost Road* 'were intimately connected; they arose at the same time and from the same impulse, and my father worked on them together' (*ibid.* p.9). I came therefore to the conclusion that '"Númenór" (as a distinct and formalized conception, whatever "Atlantis-haunting", as my father called it, lay behind) arose in the actual context of his discussions with C.S. Lewis in (as seems probable) 1936.'

In the first of the two texts of *The Fall of Númenor* there occurs this passage:

[when] ... Morgoth was thrust again into the Outer Darkness, the Gods took counsel. The Elves were summoned to Valinor ... and many obeyed, but not all.

But in the second version this was changed to read:

But when Morgoth was thrust forth, the Gods held council. The Elves were summoned to return into the West, and such as obeyed dwelt again in Eressëa, the Lonely Island, which was renamed Avallon: for it is hard by Valinor.

This is one of the first occurrences of the name *Avallon* for *Eressëa.* In the fragmentary narrative of the Númenórean story for *The Lost Road* that was all that my father ever wrote of it Elendil tells his son Herendil:

And they [the Valar] recalled the Exiles of the Firstborn and pardoned them; and such as returned dwell since in bliss in Eressëa, the Lonely Isle, which is Avallon, for it is within sight of Valinor and the light of the Blessed Realm.

To this time, it may be supposed, belongs an entry in *The Etymologies* (an extremely difficult working text from this period published in *The Lost Road and Other Writings*) under the stem LONO- (p.370):

> *lóna* : island, remote land difficult to reach. Cf. *Avalóna* = *Tol Eressëa* = the outer isle. [Probably added subsequently: *A-val-lon.*]

Another entry that bears on this name, under the stem AWA-, reads (in part):

> away, forth; out. Q[uenya] *ava* outside, beyond. *Avakúma* Exterior Void beyond the World. [To this was added: *Avalóna,* cf. *lóna.*]

These etymologies do not accord with the explanation of the name ('hard by Valinor') in the second version of *The Fall of Númenor.*

At this time, when my father was pondering the successive tales that were to constitute *The Lost Road*, but of which only fragments would ever be told, he wrote down at great speed a note on the possibility of a story of 'the man who got onto the Straight Road'. That man would be Ælfwine, the Englishman of the tenth century of whom my father had written much in earlier years: the mariner who came to the Lonely Isle and there learned from the Elves the histories that are set out in *The Book of Lost Tales*. I give here my father's note:

> But this would do best of all for introduction to the Lost Tales: How Ælfwine sailed the Straight Road. They sailed on, on, on over the sea; and it becme very bright and very calm – no clouds, no wind. The water seemed thin and white below. Looking down Ælfwine suddenly saw lands and mountains [*or* a mountain] down in the water shining in the sun. Their breathing difficulties. His companions dive overboard one by one. Ælfwine falls insensible when he smells a marvellous fragrance as of land and flowers. He awakes to find the ship being drawn by people walking in the water. He is told very few men there in a thousand years can breathe air of Eressëa (which is Avallon), but *none* beyond. So he comes to Eressëa and is told the Lost Tales.

It is interesting to compare this with the conclusion of *The Silmarillion* in the version entitled *Quenta Silmarillion*, the form of the work before my father laid it aside during *The Lord of the Rings* years (*The Lost Road and Other Writings*, pp.333–5). Here the name *Avallon* for Tol Eressëa had entered, but not yet the conception of the Straight Road.

153

Here endeth *The Silmarillion*: which is drawn out in brief
from those songs and histories which are yet sung and told
by the fading Elves, and (more clearly and fully) by the
vanished Elves that dwell now upon the Lonely Isle, Tol
Eressëa, whither few mariners of Men have ever come, save
once or twice in a long age when some man of Eärendel's
race hath passed beyond the lands of mortal sight and seen
the glimmer of the lamps upon the quays of Avallon, and
smelt afar the undying flowers in the meads of Dorwinion.
Of whom was Eriol one, that men named Ælfwine, and he
alone returned and brought tidings of Cortirion [city of the
Elves in Eressëa] to the Hither Lands.

There is no need to pursue the subject of *Avallon* into the
complexities of later development, which are fully recounted in
Sauron Defeated (1992). I have attempted in this summary only
to suggest what that name meant to my father in the context of
'The Silmarillion' at the time when he was working on *The Fall
of Arthur*, and probably nearing its abandonment.

It seems to me that one should assume a considerable
passage of time for the emergence of so huge a perturba-
tion of the existing myth, brought about by the irruption of
Númenor and its drowning, the elemental refashioning of
the earth, and the mystery of the 'Straight Path' leading to a
vanished 'past' denied to mortals. I think therefore that it is at
least quite probable that this evolution in 'The Silmarillion',
together with the new enterprise of *The Lost Road* and the
severe doubts and difficulties that my father encountered,

were in themselves sufficient to account for his turning away from *The Fall of Arthur*.

This would indeed argue a surprisingly late date for its abandonment, but there is in fact a very curious and puzzling piece of evidence which seems to support this supposition. This is a single page of very rough notes, a list of successive 'elements' in the narrative, all of which are found elsewhere. The latter part of the list reads thus:

> Battle of Camlan
> Arthur slays Mordred
> & is wounded
> *Aug 1937* | Carried to Avalon
> Lancelot arrives too late
> [? rejoins] Queen
> Goes in ship West and is never heard of again

At some time after this list was made my father entered the bracket that separates 'Carried to Avalon' from what precedes, and against the bracket (i.e. on the same line as 'Carried to Avalon') wrote 'Aug 1937'.

The most natural way, perhaps, to interpret this is that my father had reached (in verse, if not in polished form) 'Arthur slays Mordred and is wounded', but no further, at that time. The problem with that, of course, is that he had not even reached the Battle of Camlan: the poem ceases with the end of the fighting at Romeril, and the manuscript evidence gives no indication that verse-form ever extended any further. I cannot explain this. But at least there seems to be evidence here that my father was still actively concerned with *The Fall of Arthur* in August 1937, surprisingly late as that seems.

But if this were the case, is any light cast thereby on the question, why did he at about this time write that *Tol Eressëa*, a name then going back some twenty years, was changed to *Avallon* – for no very evident reason? That there was no connection at all with the Arthurian Avallon seems impossible to accept; but it must be said that similarity to the departure of Arthur became still less evident.

In a letter of September 1954, after the publication of *The Fellowship of the Ring*, my father wrote a beautifully brief and lucid statement concerning Eressëa:

> ... Before the Downfall there lay beyond the sea and the west-shores of Middle-earth an *earthly* Elvish paradise Eressëa, and *Valinor* the land of the *Valar* (the Powers, the Lords of the West), places that could be reached physically by ordinary sailing-ships, though the Seas were perilous. But after the rebellion of the Númenóreans, the Kings of Men, who dwelt in a land most westerly of all mortal lands, and eventually in the height of their pride attempted to occupy Eressëa and Valinor by force, Númenor was destroyed, and Eressëa and Valinor removed from the physically attainable Earth: the way west was open, but led nowhere but back again – for mortals.

It seems to me that the most that can be said is that the Fortunate Isle, the Avalon of Morgan la Fée, and the Avallon that was Tol Eressëa, are associated only in that they both have the character of an 'earthly paradise' far over the western ocean.

Nonetheless, there is good reason, indeed, compelling evidence, to believe that my father did expressly make this connection, although the underlying motive may be difficult to interpret.

Among my father's notes for the continuation of *The Fall of Arthur* the one that tells Lancelot took a boat and sailed into the west, but never returned, is of particular interest in the present context on account of the words that follow and conclude the note: 'Eärendel passage' (p.136). These lines of alliterative verse, found together with the notes for the continuation of *The Fall of Arthur*, have been given on pp.137–8.

In this brief poem 'the galleon was thrust *on the shadowy seas*', and Eärendel 'goeth *to magic islands* ... past the hills of Avalon ... *the dragon's portals and the dark mountains / of the Bay of Faery beyond the borders of the world.*' In these lines my father was expressly introducing elements of the mythical geography of the First Age of the World as originally described in *The Book of Lost Tales*, but which largely survived into much later texts of 'The Silmarillion'.

In the tale of 'The Hiding of Valinor' in *The Book of Lost Tales Part I* it is told that in the time of the fortification of Valinor the Magic Isles were set in a great ring in the ocean as a defence of the Bay of Faëry. By the time of the version of 'The Silmarillion' entitled *The Quenta*, written or largely written in 1930, this was said (*The Shaping of Middle-earth*, 1986, p.98):

157

In that day, which songs call The Hiding of Valinor, the Magic Isles were set, filled with enchantment, and strung across the confines of the Shadowy Seas, before the Lonely Isle is reached sailing West, there to entrap mariners and wind them in everlasting sleep.

It is notable that the expression 'the Bay of Faery on the borders of the world' in the last line of the 'Eärendel passage' is found frequently in early writings. It constitutes the fourth line in the second version of the alliterative poem *The Children of Húrin*, in or before 1925 (*The Lays of Beleriand*, 1985, p.95):

> Ye Gods who girt   your guarded realms
> with moveless pinnacles,   mountains pathless,
> o'er shrouded shores   sheer uprising
> of the Bay of Faëry   on the borders of the World!

In *The Quenta* all these names appear together in the story of Eärendel (*The Shaping of Middle-earth*, p.150). On their voyage to Valinor bearing the Silmaril Eärendel and Elwing in the ship *Wingelot*

> came unto the Magic Isles, and escaped their magic; and they came into the Shadowy Seas and passed their shadows; and they looked upon the Lonely Isle and they tarried not there; and they cast anchor in the Bay of Faërie upon the borders of the world.

Particularly striking are the words 'the dragon's portals' in the penultimate verse of the 'Earendel passage'. In the tale of 'The Hiding of Valinor' it is told (*The Book of Lost Tales Part I*, pp.215–16) that the Gods 'dared a very great deed, the most mighty of all their works':

'They drew to the Wall of Things, and there they made the Door of Night.... There it still stands, utterly black and huge against the deep-blue walls. Its pillars are of the mightiest basalt and its lintel likewise, but great dragons of black stone are carved thereon, and shadowy smoke pours slowly from their jaws. Gates it has unbreakable, and none know how they were made or set, for the Eldar were not suffered to be in that dread building, and it is the last secret of the Gods.'

(The expressions 'dragonheaded door' and 'Night's dragon-headed doors' are found in early poems: *The Book of Lost Tales Part II*, pp.272, 274.)

In this earliest form of the astronomical myth 'the galleon of the Sun' passes through the Door of Night, 'goes out into the limitless dark, and coming behind the world finds the East again', returning through the Gates of Morn. But this conception was early overtaken by a new form of the myth, in which the Sun does not enter the Outer Dark by the Door of Night but passes beneath the Earth. The Door of Night remained, but changed in purpose and the time of its making. In the brief work named *Ambarkanta*, The Shape of the World, of 1930 or a little later, the new significance of the Door of Night is expressed in these passages (*The Shaping of Middle-earth*, pp.235, 237):

About all the World are the Ilurambar, or Walls of the World. They are as ice and glass and steel, being above all imagination of the Children of Earth cold, transparent, and hard. They cannot be seen, nor can they be passed, save by the Door of Night.

Within these Walls the Earth is globed: above, below, and upon all sides is Vaiya, the Enfolding Ocean.

In the midst of Valinor is *Ando Lómen*, the Door of Timeless Night that pierceth the Walls and opens upon the Void. For the World is set amid Kúma, the Void, the Night without form or time. But none can pass the chasm and the belt of Vaiya and come to that Door, save the great Valar only. And they made that Door when Melko [Morgoth] was overcome and put forth into the Outer Dark; and it is guarded by Eärendel.

I have of course set out here all these passages, chosen from an immense body of writing, not for their own intrinsic significance, but to reinforce the remarkable nature of my father's deliberate and substantial evocation of a cardinal myth of his own 'world', the great voyage of Eärendel to Valinor, in relation to Sir Lancelot of Arthurian legend – to whom, indeed, he was now ascribing a great voyage across the western ocean.*

---

* In this connection it may be recalled that (though with a query) Gawain's ship was named *Wingelot*, Foam-flower, the name of Eärendel's ship (p.129).

It will be observed that in these lines of the 'Eärendel passage' (pp.137–8) the only name that does not derive from the 'Silmarillion' narratives is *the hills of Avalon*. Comparing the description of the voyage of Eärendel and Elwing in the quotation from *The Quenta* given on p.158, where after the passage of the Shadowy Seas and the Magic Isles 'they looked upon the Lonely Isle and they tarried not there', it seems at least very probable that 'Avalon' here bears the meaning 'Tol Eressëa', as in the texts of the 1930s cited on pp.151–2. If this is so, then where my father wrote in a 'Silmarillion' context that *Tol Eressëa* was renamed *Avallon*, he also wrote *Avalon* for *Tol Eressëa* in an Arthurian context.

It may be thought that the 'Eärendel verses' show no more than a large parallel between two great westward voyages. But the second poem, in the first phase of composition and extraordinarily difficult to read (and with two most unfortunate illegibilities), found among these papers* and given on pp.138–9, introduces much more extraordinary associations.

These verses open with the reflection that while Gawain's grave lies 'by the sounding sea, where the sun westers' there are no burial mounds of Lancelot or Guinevere, and 'no mound hath Arthur in mortal land' – and the verses that follow concern Arthur: but they are very closely similar, or nearly identical, to the concluding lines of the 'Eärendel

---

* Very primitive drafting for the opening lines is in fact found on one of the pages of the notes for the continuation of *The Fall of Arthur*.

verses'. It is not immediately obvious which of these two 'poems', for convenience here called *Eärendel's Quest* and *Arthur's Grave*, preceded the other. It might seem that the much more finished form, in typescript, of *Eärendel's Quest* suggests that it is the later; but the fact that the names closely associated with the Eärendel legend accompany the figure of Eärendel in that poem, whereas in *Arthur's Grave* those names are associated with King Arthur, seems to me a stronger argument that *Arthur's Grave* followed *Eärendel's Quest*.

It is said at the end of *Arthur's Grave* that Arthur 'bides' (changed from 'sleeps') in Avalon, while the Bay of Faëry becomes the Bay of Avalon. On the face of it, Arthur's living presence 'in Avalon' suggests that the name is here used in the familiar Arthurian sense of the island to which Arthur was taken to be healed by Morgan La Fée; but its appearance in the context of 'Silmarillion' names seems also to indicate that it was Tol Eressëa.

Similar is the change of the name of the Bay of Elvenhome (or of Faërie, or of Eldamar) to the Bay of Avalon. The name Avalon, now used of Tol Eressëa, is here extended from the isle to the coasts of the vast bay in which Tol Eressëa was anchored.*

It seems then that the Arthurian *Avalon*, the Fortunate Isle, *Insula Pomorum*, dominion of Morgan la Fée, had now been in some mysterious sense identified with Tol Eressëa,

---

* In the original story the Lonely Isle was anchored in the mid-ocean, and no land could be seen 'for many leagues' sail from its cliffs': this was the reason for the name.

the Lonely Isle. But the name *Avallon* entered, as a name of Tol Eressëa, at the time when the Fall of Númenor and the Change of the World entered also (see pp.151–2), with the conception of the Straight Path out of the Round World that still led to Tol Eressëa and Valinor, a road that was denied to mortals, and yet found, in a mystery, by Ælfwine of England.

How my father saw this conjunction I am wholly unable to say. It may be that through absence of more precise dating I have been led to combine into a contemporaneous whole ideas that were not coherent, but emerged and fell aside in that time of great creative upheaval. But I will repeat here what I said in *The Lost Road and Other Writings*, p.98, of my father's intentions for his 'time-travel' book:

> With the entry at this time of the cardinal ideas of the Downfall of Númenor, the World Made Round, and the Straight Road, into the conception of 'Middle-earth', and the thought of a 'time-travel' story in which the very significant figure of the Anglo-Saxon Ælfwine would be both 'extended' into the future, into the twentieth century, and 'extended' also into a many-layered past, my father was envisaging a massive and explicit linking of his own legends with those of many other places and times: all concerned with the stories and the dreams of peoples who dwelt by the coasts of the great Western Sea.

✳

In conclusion, it remains to consider those notes of my father's for the continuation of the story of Lancelot and Guinevere (pp.136–7).

We learn of Lancelot after his return, too late, from France that he rode west from Romeril 'along the empty roads', and that he met Guinevere 'coming down out of Wales'. Already the narrative was set to turn definitively from that found in the stanzaic *Morte Arthur*, which was closely followed by Malory, of whose account I gave a brief sketch on pp.114–16. My father's notes, exceedingly brief as they are, show beyond question that the later years of this Guinevere will know nothing of a nunnery, or of 'fastynge, prayers, and alme-dedis' with a long face, and she will certainly not call upon Lancelot in such words as these:

> 'But I beseche the, in alle thynge,
> That newyr in thy lyffe after thysse
> Ne come to me for no sokerynge,
> Nor send me sond, but dwelle in blysse:
> I pray to Gode euyr lastynge
> To graunt me grace to mend my mysse.'*

Still less will this Lancelot reply in such words as these of Malory's:

---

* *sokerynge* succouring, assistance; *sond* message; *mend my mysse* mend my wrongdoing.

'Now, my swete madame,' seyde sir Launcelot, 'wolde ye that I shuld turne agayne unto my contrey, and there to wedde a lady? Nay, madame, wyte you well that shall I never do, for I shall never be so false unto you of that I have promysed. But the selff [*same*] destiny that ye have takyn you to, I woll take me to, for the pleasure of Jesu, and ever for you I caste me specially to pray.'

All otherwise was their meeting when she came down from Wales as my father would tell it. It was indeed foreseen in verses of the third canto:

> Strange she deemed him,
> by a sudden sickness from his self altered.　　(III.95–6)

> Strange he deemed her
> from her self altered. By the sea stood he
> as a graven stone grey and hopeless.
> In pain they parted.　　(III.106–9)

In the stanzaic *Morte Arthur* there was great sorrow at the last meeting and the parting in the nunnery:

> But none erthely man covde telle
> The sorow that there by-gan to bene

and in Malory's tale 'there was lamentacyon as they had be stungyn with sperys' (p.115); but there was determination and resignation. In the last meeting between them in the notes to *The Fall of Arthur* (pp.136–7) there was desolation and empti- ness. In the first of the notes that bear on this Lancelot asks of Guinevere only: *Where is Arthur?* Though the mood is of course altogether different, this has something of the pared- down poignancy of Morwen's question to Húrin concerning Túrin as she died: 'If you know, tell me! *How did she find him?*' Húrin said nothing; and Guinevere had nothing to tell. Lancelot 'turned from her.'

In another note concerning their last meeting it is said that Lancelot had no love left but for Arthur: Guinevere had lost all her power over him. The words of the third canto are repeated: 'In pain they parted', but now is added 'cold and griefless'. This Lancelot is not going to spend his last years in fasting and penance, and to end his life eating and drinking so little that he 'dryed and dwyned awaye' (p.115). He went to the sea shore and learned from the hermit who dwelt there that Arthur had departed west over the ocean. He set sail to follow Arthur, and no more was ever heard of him. 'Whether he found Arthur in Avalon and will return no one knows.'

But what lay before Sir Lancelot, is declared by the poet in the concluding lines of the third canto. Though filled with a lighter mind and new hope in Benwick after the great storm had passed, 'the hour he knew not':

> The tides of chance   had turned backward,
> their flood was passed   flowing swiftly.
> Death was before him   and his day setting

beyond the tides of time   to return never
among waking men,   while the world lasted.

One may imagine that my father saw his story of the departure of Sir Lancelot as re-enacting in some sense the tale of Tuor, father of Eärendel (Tuor was the son of Huor, the brother of Húrin; he wedded Idril Celebrindal, the daughter of Turgon King of Gondolin). In the *Quenta* of 1930 this is told of him:

> In those days Tuor felt old age creep upon him, and he could not forbear the longing that possessed him for the sea; wherefore he built a great ship Eärámë, Eagle's pinion, and with Idril he set sail into the sunset and the West, and came no more into any tale.

Eärendel afterwards built *Wingelot*, and set out on a great voyage, with a double purpose: to find Idril and Tuor, who had never come back, and 'he thought to find perhaps the last shore and bring ere he died a message to the Gods and Elves of the West.' But Eärendel did not find Tuor and Idril, nor did he on that first western voyage reach the shores of Valinor.

We last see Guinevere watching from far off the sails of Lancelot's departing ship: 'she sees his silver banner vanish under the moon.' There is mention of her flight into Wales to escape from 'the men of the East.' From my father's few pencilled sentences it seems that her life henceforward held nothing but grievous loneliness and self-pity; 'but though grief was her lot it is not said that she mourned for others more than for herself.' Two lines of verse that he wrote (p.137) have the air of an epitaph.

Guinevere grew grey in the grey shadow
all things losing who at all things grasped.

*

THE EVOLUTION
OF THE POEM

THE EVOLUTION OF THE POEM

It was a remarkable feature of my father's 'Norse' poems, *The Lay of the Völsungs* and *The Lay of Gudrún*, that of work preceding the finished text there survive only a few pages, and apart from these 'there is no trace of any earlier drafting whatsoever' (*The Legend of Sigurd and Gudrún*, p.40). Obviously such material existed, and was lost at some stage. Very different indeed is the case of *The Fall of Arthur*, where there are some 120 pages of drafting (preserved, not surprisingly, in a state of confusion) preceding the 'final' text given in this book. The movement from the earliest workings (often only partly legible) can be largely followed through succeeding manuscripts that underwent abundant emendation. In some parts of the poem confusing elements are the parallel development of different versions, and the movement of blocks of text to stand in different contexts.

The amount of time and thought that my father expended on this work is astounding. It would be possible of course to provide a complete and detailed textual apparatus, including an account of every emendation that arose in the successive manuscripts as he searched unceasingly for a better rhythm, or a better word or phrase within the alliterative constraints. But this would be huge task, and in my view disproportionate.

On the other hand, to omit all textual commentary would be to conceal remarkable and essential elements of the poem's creation. This is especially so in the case of Canto III, which was the heart of the poem, the most worked upon, and the most changed in the process, and I have provided a fairly full account (fuller than might generally be thought desirable, and inevitably not at all points easy to follow) of that history as I understand it; but throughout my textual commentary on the poem I have frequently omitted minor alterations made for metrical or stylistic reasons.

In what follows I use the word 'draft' to refer to any or all of the pages of verse that precede the latest text of *The Fall of Arthur*, that is, the manuscript from which the text in this book is taken. This latest text does gives the impression of having been written as a whole and set apart, and so might be regarded as 'final', but it underwent a good deal of correction and alteration subsequently, chiefly in the first two cantos. As a rule, indeed, no manuscript of my father's could be regarded as 'final' until it had safely left his hands. But in this case by far the greater number of such changes were made quickly in pencil; and of similar changes made to the manuscripts of my father's 'Norse' poems I wrote (*The Legend of Sigurd and Gudrún*, p.40): 'I have the impression that my father read through the text many years later ... and quickly emended points that struck him as he went.' The same may well be true of *The Fall of Arthur*, but of course this cannot be determined. The fact that these changes are markedly more numerous in Cantos I and II may suggest renewed interest in the poem at some later date, which petered out.

However this manuscript is to be regarded, it must be constantly referred to, and I name it by the letters **LT**, for Latest Text.

A most extraordinary aspect of the writing of the poem is revealed in the draft pages: namely, that Canto I, the account of King Arthur's campaign into the East, so far from being the first to be written, was in fact introduced when work on the poem was well advanced.

There are two draft manuscripts of Canto II (the narrative of the news brought by the captain of the wrecked Frisian ship, and of Mordred's visit to Guinevere in Camelot), and also a single page carrying the opening of the poem. All three begin with the lines:

Dark wind came driving   over deep water,
from the South sweeping   surf upon the beaches ...

The earliest, which I will call *IIa*, has this title:

The Fall of Arthur
I
How [Mordred >] Radbod brought news and Mordred gathered
his army to stay the king's landing

The text is in essentials the same as that of Canto II in LT as printed, though with a great many differences, but goes no further than the equivalent of line II.109, in this text 'cormorants of the coast and the cold marches'.

The second, following, draft text, called *IIb*, has the same heading as *IIa* on the first page, but has the whole text of the canto, with again numerous differences though not of structure.

The single page, *IIc*, of the canto, referred to above, follows the text *IIb*, and here the heading is thus:

The Fall of Arthur

II

How the Frisian ship brought news, and Mordred gathered an
army and came to Camelot seeking the queen.

But the figure II in this heading was a later extension from I.

It is notable that when Canto I was added no new narrative elements or references were added to what had become Canto II; but this, I presume, was because my father's original plan had been to open the poem with Mordred and Guinevere, and he had not then considered any prior narrative necessary. One has only to read Canto II now, therefore, with this knowledge, to appreciate how little had been told of Arthur's absence from Britain: no more is said of the previous history than the words that Radbod, the captain of the Frisian ship, spoke to Mordred before he died (the

THE EVOLUTION OF THE POEM

equivalence in the draft manuscript *IIb* of the lines II.70–77 in the latest version):

> Cradoc the accurséd   hath thy counsel bewrayed, [*betrayed*]
> in Arthur's ears   all is rumoured
> of thy deeds and purpose.   Dark is his anger.
> He hastens home,   and his host summons
> from the Roman marches,   riding like a tempest.

Mordred's warning to Guinevere, II.144–7, was present in *IIb* in this form, with a reference to Benwick:

> Never again shall Arthur   enter this kingdom,
> nor Lancelot du Lake   love remembering
> from Benwick to Britain   over broad waters
> return to thy tryst!

Another, and notable, reference to Lancelot appears in *IIb* (repeated from *IIa*), where Mordred summons to his side 'lords and earls ... faithful in falseness, foes of Arthur, lovers of Lancelot': in LT (the latest text) *Lancelot* was changed to *treason* (II.105).

*

Canto III

For a number of reasons it is clearest, or at any rate least unclear, to begin this account with Canto III, 'Of Sir Lancelot, who abode in Benwick'.

The draft manuscripts consist very largely of verses, but among them are three synopses of the story of Lancelot and Guinevere as my father thought to tell it, or rather to assume it, in his poem. They were numbered (subsequently) I, II, and III. All three were written very rapidly but seldom illegibly. I have expanded contractions and made a few very minor emendations.

Synopsis I opens with a passage in praise of Lancelot that was quite closely followed in III.19–28. Then follows:

Gawain alone was almost his equal but of sterner mood, loving the king above men and above women, in courtesy cloaking mistrust of the Queen. But the Queen loved Lancelot, to his praise only would she listen. Thus jealousy awoke in lesser hearts, but most in Mordred's whom her beauty inflamed. Lancelot rejoiced in the Queen's beauty and served her ever but was loyal long to his lord, but the net closed about him and the Queen would not release him, but with laughter or with tears bent his purpose till he fell from loyalty.

Gawain guessed not but Mordred watched. At length Mordred told Gawain and his brothers Agravain and Gareth and said that as they were of the king's kin they should warn him. Agravain jealous of Lancelot's estate and favour on his brother's behalf told the king. The court was rent with feud. [*Added*: Agravain slain by Lancelot.] Mordred told Guinevere and Lancelot that the betrayal was by Gawain's purpose out of envy, and Lancelot believed the lie – though Gawain was in truth the one of all the knights who was not envious and thought only of the king and not himself. The king condemned the Queen to [*illegible word struck out and replaced by* and Lancelot to die] and men accused Lancelot of cravenhood since he had fled. But as the Queen was led to the stake Lancelot appeared at the head of his kindred and rescued her and carried her off. Gareth [? and others] of Gawain's kin were slain. But Lancelot's mood sickened and he returned the Queen – but Arthur would not look on him again and he went back to Benwick.

Neither he nor his kindred fought any more for Arthur, not even when they heard of the attacks on Britain, nor of Arthur's sortie East. This chafed his followers and they mourned for his mood – repenting penitence and his humbled pride after losing himself for love and now love for loyalty spurned.

Now word came of Mordred's treachery – and Arthur arming against his own kingdom. Lancelot saw clearer the guile he was ensnared in. Half he thought of gathering his host to help Arthur. Then pride withheld him and the thought of Gawain whom he had wronged and his cold scorn. He thought he would go nonetheless if the king called. Where was Guinevere – he had not the might to go to Britain without joining with Arthur. Was she fair and false as men said (and Mordred)? Lightly she had left him and seemed not to pity his anguish or comprehend his penitence. If she sent to tell him of peril he would come. But no word came from Arthur whom Gawain guided. No word came fom Guinevere who waited upon the times. Lancelot went not forth, but abode in Benwick. The sun shone out after storm and his heart lightened. He called for music and bade men be merry for life has still hope, but he knew not that the tides of chance had changed and he had missed the flood.

Synopsis II begins with a fairly close repetition of the opening of Synopsis I, as far as 'his will was bent and he fell from loyalty'. Then follows:

Gawain guessed but Mordred watched. Thus came the feud and the sundering of the Round Table which many have sung. [*Illegible word*] first cloud gathered over the glory of Arthur. Mordred moving darkly warns both Lancelot and the king. The king's great anger, which Gawain tries to temper, but Mordred has for the time the king's ear. He vows that both Lancelot and Guinevere shall suffer death for treason – according indeed to just law. But Lancelot warned has taken Guinevere and fled to safety (this as Mordred intended) proclaiming guilt. In the attack on the castle many are slain including Agravain and Gareth, Gawain's kinsmen. Only then will Gawain join in. He challenges Lancelot, that no more noble knights be slain. But Lancelot's mood has changed: he repents the ruin he has wrought, and the Queen is frightened and unwilling to risk the peril of Lancelot's failure. First blow to Lancelot's love. Lancelot therefore treats and yields Guinevere on condition that she shall be pardoned and received in full honour. But the king will not pardon Lancelot – nor does Gawain urge it – and banishes him, and he departs with his kindred to Benwick.

Beside the number III of the third synopsis my father noted 'followed in poem'. This begins with a greatly reduced version of the openings of the previous two synopses, and there is a good deal of repetition from synopsis I in the concluding passage, but I will cite this text in full.

Lancelot was deemed doughtiest of Arthur's knights, and the fairest of all men – dark and splendid beside the gold of Gawain. Gawain only was almost his equal, but sterner in mood, and he loved the king only above men and above women, but mistrusted the Queen even ere the shadow fell. But the Queen loved Lancelot, and Lancelot rejoiced in the Queen's beauty and served her ever gladly, and loved her above women and above men. Honour and renown only loved he almost as dear. Therefore long was he loyal to his lord. But the net closed on him, and the Queen drew the toils ever tighter – for she released seldom that which she had or ceased to grasp for what she desired. Fair as fay-woman but fell-minded in the world walking for the woe of men. Thus with smiles and tears she bent Lancelot's will.

Thus came the feud that many have sung and the first cloud over the glory of Arthur, when swords were drawn in the king's house and brethren of the Round Table slew one another. [*Struck out:* Mordred contrived it, envying Lancelot, desiring the Queen, he betrayed Lancelot.] With cruel justice the Queen was condemned to the fire, but Lancelot rescued her and carried [her] afar. That day fell many knights by the hand of Ban's kindred, and among them Gawain's brother. But his mood sickened and the

179

Queen disliked exile. He repented the slayings and returned the Queen – obtaining full pardon for her; but not for himself. He departed to Benwick with his kin and went no more to war with Arthur.

But word came of Mordred's treachery and of Arthur arming against his own kingdom. Half he resolved to gather his host and haste to the king. Pride withheld him, and the thought of the cold scorn of Gawain whom he had wronged. The king would summon him, if he had need. In thought of Guinevere anguish took him. Was she in danger – but he had no might to go to Britain without joining Arthur. Was she false as fair as some rumoured? Lightly she had left him with little pity. If she sent to him he would go at all peril against Mordred or Arthur. But no word came from Arthur who leaned on Gawain. No word came from Guinevere who waited upon the times to snatch the best from ruin. Therefore Lancelot abode in the tower of Ban torn in mind. The storm fell. The sun shone forth and his heart lifted. He told himself that life yet held hope, tides change, but he knew not that the tides of time had passed their flood and that he had missed his chance.

✽

The evolution of Canto III can to a large extent be followed in the draft papers, although there are uncertainties that I have been unable to resolve. Some primary workings survive, among them pages at a level of illegibility that can only be interpreted at all from knowledge of subsequent texts; but it is notable that even when composing at this speed my father was capable of doing so within the alliterative and metrical patterns.

Following these is a series of manuscripts proceeding in my father's common fashion, each one taking up the changes made to the previous one and then emended in its turn. The first of these, which I will call **A**, is evidently his first writing out of a text, though far from complete, of the canto. This is in rough but legible form, still with many uncertainties and substitutions as he wrote. The text begins (III.19 ff.):

> Sir Lancelot   lord of Benwick
> of old was noblest   knight of Arthur ...

Beyond this, the text A can be passed by, since it was soon (as I judge) overtaken by another manuscript, and noteworthy features in A reappear in this substantial and complex text, **B**[*].

This manuscript opens with two pages, obviously written at the same time, neither with a title, and identical at almost all points save in the opening passage of the canto. In one of these, which I will call **B 1**, the opening is thus:

> In Benwick the blessed   once Ban was king,
> whose fathers aforetime   over fallow waters
> in the holy lands   their homes leaving
> to the western world   wandering journeyed,

---

[*] A remarkable note appears in the margin of A (only) against the words *fair as fay-woman*, line III.75, where my father wrote *fair and faultless* (the latter word being perfectly clear).

Christendom bearing,   kingdoms founding,
walls uprearing   against the wild peoples.
Towers strong and tall   turned to northward
had Ban builded;   breakers thundered
loud below them   in the looming shadows
of cavernous cliffs.   Crowned with sunlight,
walled with splendour,   wind-encompassed,
they watched the waters: war they feared not.

In the other manuscript page, **B 2,** the opening is the same, word for word, as that of LT (*'the Latest Text'*) III.1–10:

In the South from sleep   to swift fury
a storm was stirred,   striding northward
over leagues of water   loud with thunder
and roaring rain   it rushed onward;
their hoary heads   hills and mountains
tossed in tumult   on the towering seas.
On Benwick's beaches   breakers pounding
ground gigantic   grumbling boulders
with ogre anger.   The air was salt
with spume and spindrift   splashed to vapour.

After these different openings to the canto both manuscripts continue with 'There Lancelot over leagues of sea ...' as in the final text, but they differ from it where that has (III.14–18):

Dark slowly fell.   Deep his anguish.
He his lord betrayed   to love yielding,

and love forsaking   lord regained not;
faith was refused him   who had faith broken,*
by leagues of sea   from love sundered.

In their place both B 1 and B 2 have:

Dark slowly fell.   Deep his anguish,
repenting repentance   and his pride humbled,
that loyalty leaving   at love's calling
he had love now lost   loyalty seeking.

A passage on a separate page is marked for substitution at this point in B2, after the words 'Deep his anguish':

he had left loyalty   at love's calling;
his loyalty no longer   his lord trusted,
his love was forsaken   beyond leagues of sea.

After the opening pages B 1 and B 2 the text continues without duplication for some distance, and can therefore be called simply B. There are a number of cases where LT differs from B, as follows (many of these instances are found in A also). The line-references in each case are to the readings of Canto III in LT as printed in this book.

---

*   In LT ('*the Latest Text*') this line read *to faith returning he was faith denied,* corrected in pencil to *faith was refused him who had faith broken.*

(III.46–53)   he long was loyal   to his lord Arthur,
              nobly striving.   But the net was strong
              that caught him captive.   The Queen held it,
              and the silken toils   slowly tighter
              drew about him.   Dear she loved him ...

The final version ('among the Round Table's royal order ...') is given on another page of the B manuscript as an alternative; and a further alternative is suggested for III.53, 'darkly hoarded. Dear she loved him':

              dearer deemed them   darkly hoarded
              kept and counted   as the Queen's treasure
              locked in dungeon.   Dear she loved him

(III.57–9)   Fate sent her forth.   Few things she loosed
             her desire seized on.   As the sun at morning ...

For the meaning compare Synopis III, 'She released seldom that which she had' (p.179).

(III.62)   steel well-tempered.   Strong will she bent.

The original reading here, in the manuscript A, was 'Strength was broken.' Against 'Strong will she bent' in B marginal readings are 'Strong her purpose' and 'Swords she broke'. LT as written had 'Strong oaths she broke', changed in pencil to 'Strong oaths they broke'.

(After III.67, later marked for omission)

Many a minstrel   mournful singing
of that time hath told,   of trust broken,
friends divided   and faith darkened.

(III.74–8)
There Ban's kindred   with blood reddened
the house of Arthur   high and golden.
The Queen was taken.   With cruel justice
fair as fay-woman   they to fire doomed her;
to death they doomed her.   But her doom came not.
Lo! Lancelot,   lightning kindled,
radiant, deadly,   riding thunder

(III.82–3) Where LT has

Gaheris and Gareth   Gawain's brethren
by the fire fell they   as fate willed it

B has a single line, later struck through:

there Gareth died,   dear to Gawain.

(III.88–90)   He mourned too late
in ruth for the ruin   of the Round Table,
the fellowship and freedom   of his fair brethren,
for Gareth grieving,   Gawain's kinsman –

unarmed he slew him,   by ill fortune,
love requiting   as he least purposed.

The last three lines of this passage were struck out at the same
time as was the previous reference to Gareth (and in the preceding text A they were bracketed for exclusion). As a result of
these deletions Gaheris and Gareth were not mentioned in LT
as written, but the lines III.82–3 were added in pencil.

(III.90–2)   His pride he repented,   his prowess cursing,
for the love yet longing   of his lord Arthur;
he would heal yet honour   .....

(After III.101)
and many saw she   whose mood darkened,
[> hardened]
who Lancelot   with love guarded, [> tended]
but to kingless queen,   captive rescued,
were she fair as fay,   friendship showed not.

(III.102)   For 'With searing words' B has 'With soft speeches',
but 'with searing words' was the reading of A.

(III.104–8) The toils she weened   for a time slackened
still in hand she held   though his heart wavered.
Other times would come.   Yet it irked waiting
and she stung him keenly.   Strange he deemed her
from her self altered.   Then sudden in vision
for a moment's anguish   as in mirror naked

her soul seeing and his self knowing
he stricken as stone stood there silent.

(After III.119)
Pride few pitied from its peak fallen,
and Gawain doubted his good purpose.
His return forbade they, unless trial sought he,
standing meekly before stern justice.

(III.124–7) Grief knew Arthur
in his heart's secret that his halls regained
wife unfaithful and more worthy missed,
his noblest knight in his need losing.

Shortly after this the text B divides again into two, and at the
point (III.143) where LT moves on to

From western havens word was rumoured
of Arthur arming against his own kingdom

these further twinned texts return, surprisingly, to the opening
passages of the canto in B 1 and B 2 (pp.181–2), with their
placing reversed, that is to say, in the manuscript where the
canto opens with 'In Benwick the blessed once Ban was king'
there appears here the passage beginning 'In the South from
sleep in swift fury', while in the other manuscript the reverse
is the case. In both versions the passage in question is followed
by the verses telling of Lancelot gazing from a window over the
sea (cf. III.11–14, 187–9):

Thence now Lancelot   over leagues of sea
in heaving welter   from a high window
looked and wondered   alone musing
doubtful-hearted.   Dark slowly fell.

(where the other manuscript has 'Dark had fallen').

My father seems to have decided eventually that of all these arrangements the most satisfactory was to retain 'In the South from sleep   to swift fury' as the opening of the canto, and that there was no place for the passage beginning 'Benwick the blessed'. See further on this p.192.

From here the B text continues with 'From western havens   word was rumoured' (III.143) in two successive forms, labelled 'Version A' and 'Version B'. I give here differences in Version A (before emendation) from LT. It is clearest to set out the text of Version A from its beginning; this corresponds to III.143–173, but the passage III.148–157 is absent.

From western havens   word had hastened
[*struck out*: of lords in Logres   leagued in treason],
of Arthur arming   against his own kingdom;
how a mighty navy   manned with vengeance
he swift assembled,   that the sudden fury
of striding storm   stayed and hindered,
beaten backward   by rebellious seas.
Now half he hoped   and half wished not
to receive summons   swift and urgent
to his king allegiance   leal [*loyal*] recalling

of Lancelot   to his lord Arthur.
To Guinever again   as to glad sunlight
thrust often back   his thought wandered.
There was war in Britain,   wild deeds were wrought –
was she false yet further   to her faith renewed
or did danger press her?   Dear he loved her.
Long she had left him,   as were love ended,
in wrath and ruin,   no ruth showing,
no pity feeling,   proud and scornful.
Dear he loved her.   If danger threatened,
if she sent him summons   he would sail at night
against foe or tempest   through furious seas
to lands forlorn   as his lady bade him.

From this point Version A is the same as LT, from III.174 to
the end of the canto, with a few minor variations:

(III.174–6) But there came neither   from his king command
　　　　　　nor word from lady;   only wind hurried
　　　　　　over wide waters   wild and voiceless.

(III.179)　ere his blood reddens   the brim of evening

(III.187)　And Lancelot   over leagues of wind

(After III.194)
　　　　　　waves white-crested   washed receding

(III.204)   high whitewingéd,   but on hills and dales

The following are differences in Version B from LT. The passage III.148–157 was absent, as in version A, but the text corresponding to III.157 ff. is distinct both from Version B and LT.

of striding storm   stayed and hindered;
beaten backward   by rebellious seas
it was held in harbour.   With heart in twain
now half he hoped,   and half wished not,
to receive summons   swift and urgent
to king his allegiance   leal recalling
of Lancelot   to his lord Arthur.
Yet pride pricked him   prayer only
to hear and answer   humbly spoken.
But there came neither   claim nor entreaty,
prayer nor order.   Pride was wounded.
In his mind saw he   men that eyed him,
and Gawain's glance   gleaming coldly,
forgiving gravely   grief that he wrought him.
So horn he blew not   nor his host gathered
though his heart was heavy   with half-purpose,
and his mood they mourned   who most loved him.
He waited and went not.   Wild roared the sea.
The towers trembled   tempest-shaken.
To Guinever again   as to glad sunlight
as from deep dungeon   and its dark prison
thrust often down   his thought wandered.

Wild deeds were wrought;   there was war in Britain –
was she false yet further   to her faith renewed
or did danger press her?

This passage then continues as in Version A, as cited above, and
continues to the end of the canto with no significant differences
from A.

*

A further complete manuscript of Canto III, which may be
called C, again without title or canto-number, is found in the
collection of draft papers, as well and legibly written as the
'final' text (i.e. LT), which quite possibly it was intended to be.
In relation to the B manuscript, or manuscripts, it does in fact
almost reach the form in LT as that was written (before it too
later received further pencilled corrections): almost all the passages detailed on pp.184–7 were changed to the final form. Its
existence shows my father's readiness to build his poem layer
upon layer, copying the same or closely similar passages again
and again, which allows the movement of the work to be followed at large or in fine detail.

Here there is only one passage in this further text C that
need be expressly recorded. This is III.124–7, of which the B
text is given on p.187. C originally had here:

Grief knew Arthur
in his heart's secret;   that his halls regained
wife unfaithful   and more

My father struck these lines out as he wrote them and replaced them with

> in his heart's secret;   and his house him seemed,
> though fairest woman   in her fell beauty
> in the golden courts   was queen again,
> now less in gladness,   and its light minished,

From this the final form was reached:

> and his house him seemed
> in mirth now minished,   marred in gladness,

Lastly, beside the opening passsage of the canto in C ('In the South from sleep to swift fury ...'). my father wrote in pencil: 'Or if this is Fit I In Benwick the blessed &c.' A 'fit' is an Old English word, meaning a part or portion of a poem, which my father sometimes used, though in reference to *The Fall of Arthur* he also used 'canto'. His meaning here can only be that he had it in mind that the 'Lancelot canto' might be the first canto of the poem, in which case *In Benwick the blessed* would be the opening lines. This may well explain the two parallel pages in the manuscript B (pp.181–2), each with one or other of the two opening passages.

*

There is a further curious complication in the history of Canto III. This is a manuscript, or series of manuscript pages amid the great heap of draft papers, in which the events leading to the feud and the breaking of the fellowhip of the Round Table were to be told in a conversation betwewen Lionel and Ector, kinsmen of Lancelot, recollecting together the grievous history.

This version begins with the passage 'In Benwick the blessed   once Ban was king ...' in the form already encountered as the opening passage of the manuscript B 1 (p.181), but with a different third line: where the other text has 'in the holy lands their homes leaving / to the western world wandering journeyed' the present text has 'from the ancient East, islands seeking / in the western world, wandering journeyed'.

Very legibly written in ink with some preliminary pencilled drafting, this version carries the canto number II in pencil. I give here the text in full, following from the last line of the opening passage, 'they watched the waters: war they feared not.'

There now Lancelot,   lord of Benwick,
dark hours endured   and deep anguish.
His mood they mourned   who most loved him,
friends and kinsmen   that his fortune shared
leaving Logres   and their lord Arthur.
Lionel and Ector   alone sitting,
uncle and nephew,   the evil days
to mind recalled.   Mighty Ector,
Ban's younger son,   of his brother speaking,
of his fame and folly,   was filled with ruth.

'In former time   of our fair brethren
he was proven peerless.   Praise and glory
and men's worship   for might and honour
he ever earned him,   until evil grew
and faith divided.   Too fair the queen,
the knight too noble,   and the net too strong
that caught him captive.   Not as queen, alas!
nor as liege lady,   but than life more dear
he long loved her,   yet loyal held him
to our lord Arthur.   But love conquered.
He strove in vain   in her strong fetters,
but release won not;   and love unyielding
with tears or laughter   the true as steel
bent slowly down   to bitter sweetness.'
    Lionel answered – lord proud-hearted,
in war unwavering,   yet in wisdom cool
men's hearts he marked   and their minds' purpose:
'Yea, little I love her,   lady ruthless,
fair as fay-woman   and fell-minded,
in the world walking   for the woe of men!
Fate sent her forth.   Yet I fouler deem*
the eyes of envy   that are ever watchful,
the malice of Mordred   moving darkly
with counsel poisoned   to crooked purpose.
Lancelot he loved not   for his large renown,

---

*   These two lines 'in the world walking ... Yet I fouler deem'
replaced 'with beauty perilous, yet blame I more (the eyes of
envy ...)'.

and for the queen's favour   cursed his fortune;
Gawain he hated,   who guile despised,
high and noble,   hard in temper;
for the king loved him,   to his counsel first
of his lieges listening;   and he his lord guarded
as jealous hound doth   gentle master.
    I watched them oft.   Words he whispered
with guile to Gawain,   Guinevere accused
and Lancelot   with lies slandered
darker than the deeds were.   Dire was the anger
and grief of Gawain.   Glad was Mordred;
for to Arthur's ears   evil tidings,
harm to hearer,   hurt to speaker,
he* bluntly brought   who best loved him.
Thus Gawain earned   Guinever's hatred;
and Lancelot   to her lie holdeth
that lust and envy   loathly changed him
to evil adder – that only knight
who almost his equal   envy knew not,
who in courtesy cloaked   a cold mistrust
of the queen's beauty.   Curséd falsehood!†
There was snake in sooth,   secret crawling,
and stealthy stinging,   whom still he sees not!'
    Ector answered: 'All our kindred

---

*   Gawain; and again three lines below.

†   The earliest reading here was 'of the queen's favour. Curséd
fortune!'

must bear the blame   of that blind folly,
but Lionel only.   We little hearkened
to thy words of wisdom,   and too well loved him
for rights or reasons,   wrong defending,
and the queen's quarrel   our cause making
for love of Lancelot.   Our love endureth,
though in twain we rent   the Round Table's
freedom and fellowship,   fiercely striving.
Swift swords we drew   against sworn brethren,
ere the queen was taken.   With cruel justice
to death they doomed her.   But her death came not.
Lo! Lancelot   as lightning's flame
radiant, deadly,   riding thunder,
in sudden assault   sweeping heedless
his friends of old   felled and trampled.
[The queen he freed   and carried her afar]

The last line was struck through, and beneath it my father
wrote in pencil the words 'I was with him', presumably
uttered by Sir Ector.

Here this text, which may be called the 'Lionel and Ector
version', referred to as **LE,** ends. I feel sure that no more
was written of this telling of the tale in reported speech. It
will be seen that from the line 'Swift swords we drew against
sworn brethren', seven lines from the end, this text moves
towards that of LT in Canto III.71–80; and the last five lines
are indeed all but identical with the text both of the earliest
manuscript A and of its successor B (p.185), which reads:

to death they doomed her.   But her doom came not.
Lo! Lancelot, lightning kindled,
radiant, deadly,   riding thunder,
in sudden assault   sweeping heedless
his friends of old   felled and trampled.

If this were all the evidence available, one would say that if my father did not have B in front of him, at any rate when he reached this point in the 'Lionel and Ector version' he must have retained the passage from B in memory; and if the latter, one might speculate that he realized at this point that Lionel and Ector were becoming mere mouthpieces for the story in retrospect as he had already told it. But as will be seen shortly (pp.202 ff.), the matter is more complex.

Before turning to this, however, this new version is of particular interest in that only here, and in Synopsis I, did my father describe in any detail the machinations of Mordred. In the second synopsis (p.178) it is said only that 'Mordred moving darkly warns both Lancelot and the king'. In the third synopsis, which, my father noted, was followed in the poem, nothing is said of this at all, save in a rejected sentence (p.179) that Mordred betrayed Lancelot; but it is also said that after his return to France, when pondering his course of action, he thought of 'the cold scorn of Gawain whom he had wronged' (p.180). Of course, none of these synopses was a careful statement of a proposed narrative: rather, they were memoranda, significant 'moments' that he wished to bear in mind, and so set down in writing.

In Synopsis I, however (p.176), we learn that Mordred told Gawain and his brothers; that Agravain told the king; and that Lancelot slew Agravain. The essential element in the story there is that Mordred, lying to Lancelot and Guinevere, said that the betrayal 'was by Gawain's purpose out of envy'; and Lancelot believed Mordred. Here appears first, what was repeated in the third synopsis, Gawain's' cold scorn' for Lancelot, by whom he had been wronged.

In the 'Lionel and Ector' version of the canto, *Mordred accused Guinevere and Lancelot to Gawain*, and in 'anger and grief' *Gawain told the king*, so earning Guinevere's hatred, and her lie that Gawain had been changed by lust and envy into a snake – which Lancelot believed, and greatly wronged him.

This is a convenient place to introduce yet another text, very brief. The first of two pages was written in soft pencil, and looks as if it were dashed down as new composition, almost without punctuation; but it is surprisingly legible, though not at all points.

Lancelot was holden   by low and high
freest most fearless   of the fair brethren
of the Round Table   ere ruinous time
and Mordred's malice   mischief compassed

At this point the text is interrutpted by extraneous notes and it is not clear whether what follows is to be treated as continuous.

jealousy awakened   joy was darkened
for none would the queen   hear named in praise
save Lancelot alone   it liked them ill –
the lesser in loyalty   [*illegible*]
when Mordred's malice   moved to evil.
words were spoken   of woman's frailty
and man's weakness,   and many harkened.
The king men told   how his court was dishonoured –
[? and *or* by] Mordred   himself with mouth smiling
Yet the queen he told   that her counsel was betrayed
by Gawain the good   for his great purity
his love and loyalty   to his liege Arthur.
Thus came the hate   of Gawain and Lancelot
Thus came the hate   of Gawain and Guinever
Thus came the wrath   of Arthur and Lancelot
He left the company   of the Round Table
sailed back over sea   to his seats of old
to Joyous Gard   in the jagged hills
in Benoic the blessed   where Ban had ruled

The story of the feud arising from the love of Lancelot and
Guinevere seems here to be that Mordred told Guinevere that
Gawain had told the King.

The last two lines (at the bottom of the page) are notable
for the names. This is the only place in the *Fall of Arthur*
papers where the name *Joyous Gard* appears (see pp.99–100,
102, 116), here set 'in the jagged hills in *Benoic*' – elsewhere
always *Benwick*: but *Benoic* is the form in the French *Mort
Artu* (p.102).

The second of the two pages was written in ink in a scrawl that is very hard to decipher. It begins with the line 'Thus came the hate of Gawain and Lancelot' and repeats the following six lines (with *Benwick* for *Benoic*). Then follows:

[? So] the worm had pierced   all the wealth and root
of the Tree of blossom   in its time of [*illegible word*]
so went Lancelot no more   with his liege to battle
on the far marches   against the fierce Saxons.
[*illegible line*]
A word over the water   of woe in Britain
came to Lancelot   in his land afar
of Arthur arming   against his own kingdom.
he waited and went not.   Word from [? his] lady
came not [? him calling],   from the king no summons
to sail over salt water   was sent to him
for Gawain the good   of Guinevere's [? friends]
[*illegible words*]

These last words might be read as 'doubted as faithless'. It seems to me that this text was a very early sketching out of this element in the story. Incidentally, the lines in this text (p.199)

jealousy awakened   joy was darkened
for none would the queen   hear named in praise
save Lancelot alone   it liked them ill –
the lesser in loyalty

are reminiscent of the words of Synopsis I, p.176: 'But the Queen loved Lancelot, to his praise only would she listen. Thus jealousy awoke in lesser hearts ...'

There is also another single page that seems fairly certainly to be associated with the pages of the preceding text: it was found with them and is on the same subject, with one closely similar line. The text begins in mid-sentence, but the preceding page has disappeared; and was written very rapidly in ink.

> of Arthur arming   against his own kingdom.
> Oft he wondered   whether word would come,
> would Arthur ask him   for aid in war.
>   Now Mordred's malice   was made clear to him
> and many things he saw   he had missed before.
> Oft then we wished and wondered   that word might come
> to summon him to sail   over salt water
> asking for his aid   in Arthur's need.
> Or haply from Britain   he would hear ere long
> and the queen would call him   to comfort her.
>   But no word came   and he cursed the day
> and a black thought   brooded in his breast at eve.
> Let the king be conquered – and the queen widowed.
> [In] Mordred shall remember   the might of Benwick
> another more worthy   shall that crown seize.
>   Grim were his looks.
>   Ector said to Lionel

I don't think that these last words show that this text was associated with the abandoned device of putting the retrospective
story of Lancelot and Guinevere into the mouths of Sir Lionel
and Sir Ector. I think it belongs rather with an isolated note
in which my father proposed to himself that some part of the
earlier history should be 'worked in with Lancelot's musing
– at the rising of the storm', and should be further amplified
'when Ector and Lionel discuss his inaction and chafe at it'
(see p.208). In the line 'In Mordred shall remember' the word
'In' seems clear but is obviously an error, perhaps for 'Then'.
I assume that 'that crown' refers to the crown of Britain.
Lancelot's speculation about a possibly desirable outcome of
Britain's woes is astounding, and has no echo anywhere in
the draft papers. On the other hand, his perplexity of mind as
portrayed in Synopsis I (p.177), and similarly in Synopsis III
(p.180), could be seen as fertile ground from which so black a
'black thought' could 'brood in his breast'.

Returning to the question of the Lionel and Ector text
(LE) and its convergence with the B version (pp. 196–7), the
fact is that there exists another manuscript which is demonstrably earlier than LE, which my father was demonstrably
following when he wrote LE, but from which Lionel and
Ector are absent.

In this manuscript the *In Benwick the blessed* opening
passage is in an earlier form than in any of its numerous
other occurrences. In line 3 it has 'from the ancient East,
islands seeking', as does LE (p.193); but in addition it has the

following readings where LE has the later ones (see p.181): in line 6 'against the wilderness' for 'against the wild peoples'; in line 7 'Tower' for 'Towers' (and so 'below it' in line 9 for 'below them', 'it watched' and 'it feared' for 'they' in line 12); and 'carven cliffs' for 'cavernous cliffs' in line 10. These and many other corrections were written in the margins of this text, but I give it as it was before the corrections were made.

After the opening passage this further text continues thus, to be compared with that of LE on pp.193 ff.

> There now Lancelot,   the lord of Benwick,
> bitter days abode   burned with longing.
> In former time   of the fair brethren
> he was proven peerless;   praise and glory
> and men's worship   for might and honour
> he had ever earned him,   until evil grew
> and faith divided.   Too fair the Queen,
> the knight too noble,   and the net too strong
> that caught him captive.   Not as Queen only
> nor as lady he loved her,   but than life more dear
> he loved her long,   yet loyal held him
> to his lord Arthur.   Love was stronger.
> By her beauty blinded   he bent at last,
> trust betraying,   who was true as steel.
> Thus the seed was sown   of sorrow unending.
>   Eyes hath envy   that are ever watchful:
> most was Mordred   by malice goaded:
> he loved not Lancelot   for his large renown,

and for the queen's favour   cursed his fortune;
Gawain he hated,   great and steadfast,
strong, unbending,   stern in temper,
who the queen mistrusted   but the king worshipped
as jealous as a hound   gentle master
watches unwearied.   Words he spake then
with guile to Gawain: Guinevere accused
and Lancelot   with lies slandered
darker than the deeds were.   Dire was the anger
of Gawain the good – grief smote his heart.
Thus to Arthur's ears   evil tidings,
bitter words he brought   who best loved him.
Thus Gawain   earned Guinevere's hatred
and Lancelot's love   he lost for ever;
and Mordred watched   moved to laughter.
In twain was rent   the Round Table's
freedom and fellowship   with fierce quarrels.
Swift swords were drawn   by sworn brethren
brother brother slew,   blood spilled in wrath,
ere the queen was captive.   With cruel justice
to death they doomed her.   But the day came not.
For Lancelot   like lightning's flame
raging, deadly,   riding the thunder
in sudden assault   sweeping heedless
his friends of old   felled and sundered.
The queen he freed,   and carried her afar;
then rage left him,   and his wrath sickened,
his mood faltered.   He mourned too late

in ruth for the ruin   of the Round Table,
the fellowship and freedom   of his fair brethren,
longing yet for the love   of his lord Arthur,
repenting his pride   and his prowess even.
    Pardon was denied him.   Peace he sought for;
honour yet would heal   with his own sorrow,
and the queen's estate   with her king's mercy
establish anew.   Strange she deemed him;
yet she liked little   lonely exile
as for love to lose   her life's splendour.
Thus in pain they parted.   Pardon she was granted,
in the courts of Camelot   to be queen once more,
though Gawain grudged it.   Grace with Arthur
Lancelot found not: from the land banished,
from the Round Table   reft of knighthood,
from his height fallen   to his homes afar
he went as he would not.   Woe knew Arthur
in his heart's secret   that his halls regained
Queen surpassing fair   at cost so heavy,
his noblest knight   in his need losing.
    Not alone from the land   over loud waters
went Lancelot.   Lords of his kindred
many were and mighty.   At their masts floated
the banners of Blamore   and of Bors the strong,
of Lionel and Lavain   and loyal Ector
Ban's younger son.   These to Benwick sailed
Britain forsaking.   In battle no more
to Arthur's aid   their arms bore they,

but in the towers of Ban, tall and dauntless,
watchful dwelt they, war refusing,
Lancelot their lord with love guarding.

Here my father left a space, before continuing, as it appears, at the same time (and with line-numbering continuous with the text that preceded) and on a different subject. Later, in a smaller and more careful hand, he inserted in the margin following the words 'with love guarding':

in his days of darkness. Deep his anguish,
repenting repentance and his pride humbled,
who loyalty had left in love's service
and love had now lost loyalty craving.

It is not obvious where this text should be placed in relation to the other manuscripts of Canto III, but from various indications I think it very probable that it stands closest to the earliest of them, A (p.181) and may therefore be called as a mere convenience A*; but in any case it must be regarded as a distinct treatment, in view of the account given on how the feud came to pass, which is only found in the manuscript of the poem here and in the 'Lionel and Ector version' deriving from it (see p.198). That my father had A* in front of him when he wrote LE, and that as he wrote it he transformed it into a conversation between Lionel and Ector, is very plain. If I am correct in seeing A* as deriving from a time near to the beginning of my father's writing of the 'Lancelot canto', it would presumably follow that the idea of telling the story of Lancelot and Guinevere as a discussion between two Knights of the Round Table, kinsmen of Lancelot, was also early in the evolution of the poem, and early abandoned.

*

Canto I

I have said that the account in this manuscript A* of the feud that tore the Round Table apart is followed after a space by verses on a different subject, with continuous line-numbering. I set out here the lines of this manuscript at this point:

> In battle no more 85
> to Arthur's aid   their arms bore they,
> but in the towers of Ban,   tall and dauntless
> watchful dwelt they,   war refusing,
> Lancelot their lord   with love guarding.
>
> Arthur eastward   in arms journeyed, 90
> and war he waged   on the wild marches ...

Here is the first appearance in the draft papers of what would become the opening lines of the poem, the first lines of Canto I, Arthur's campaign against the heathen invaders from the east. That my father had always intended to give an important place in his poem to the 'eastern campaign' of King Arthur seems very unlikely. There is only one reference to it in the synopses: this is in synopsis I (p.177), 'Neither he [Lancelot] nor his kindred fought any more for Arthur, not even when they heard of the attacks on Britain, nor of Arthur's sortie East.' There are also some pencilled notes on an isolated slip of paper suggesting structural orderings of the cantos. One of these reads:

I Arthur Eastward
II Lancelot and the rising storm [*followed by an illegible reference to Guinevere*]
III Mordred

The other reads:

II   Make Arthur's eastward journey immediately after Flight of Guinevere
III Work in part of back history with Lancelot musing – at rising of storm. [? More] when Ector and Lionel discuss his inaction and chafe at it
IV Romeril and Death of Gawain

These sequences, agreeing neither with each other nor with the structure of the poem in the latest text, probably reflect my father's own musings when Arthur's eastern campaign had appeared as a chief element in the narrative. In the remark on Canto III in the second group of notes he is seen reflecting on the mode in which the story in retrospect of Lancelot and Guinevere and the great feud is to be framed. Note II in the second group is hard to interpret.

I have to admit that while the sequence of composition in repect of the manuscripts of individual cantos can be worked out, I have found it impossible to detect with certainty the sequence in which these structural movements took place. But from the surviving draft material, which is sufficiently abundant, it does seem at least very probable that it was here, in the manuscript A*, suddenly, 'unheralded' as it were, that the great assault by King Arthur on the barbarians made its entry into *The Fall of Arthur*.

The relation between this earliest surviving manuscript of Canto I 'How Arthur & Gawain went to war and rode into the East', which is the the latter part of A* but which I will distinguish as **AE**, for 'Arthur Eastward', and the final text, is extraordinary. I give here the text of AE for the first 28 lines, with the line-numbers of the (more or less) corresponding verses in LT (the Latest Text) given in the margin.

Arthur eastward   in arms journeyed   (I.1–4)
and war he waged   on the wild marches
over seas sailing   to Saxon lands,
from the Roman realm   ruin defending.
Halls and temples   of the heathen kings   (I.41–2)
his might assailed   marching in conquest
to misty Mirkwood's   margin dreary. *(After I.43, struck out)*

The following eight lines were inserted into the text, at the time of writing, with a direction to place them after line 7:

Thus the tides of time   to turn backward,   (I.5–9)
heathen men to tame   his heart purposed,
that with harrying fleets   they should hunt no more
on the shining shores   and shallow waters

of Southern Britain seeking booty,
raiding and ravaging. Ravens croaking   (I.76–8)
the eagles answered in the air wheeling,
wolves were howling on the wood's border.

Lancelot he missed; Lionel and Ector,   (I.44–5)
Bors and Blamore to battle came not.
But the times drave him and treacherous fate,
and Mordred's malice moved his counsels.
Gawain guessed not guile or treason,   (I.35)
in war rejoicing; worship seeking
before the foremost fiercely rode he
[*struck out:* his king's bulwark.] Cold blew the wind. (I.79)
From the west came word winged and urgent   (I.143–5)
of war awaking and woe in Britain.
Careworn came Cradoc the king seeking,
riding restless; rent were his garments,
with haste and hunger his horse foundered.

If one compared these two texts without any other knowledge
one might suppose that the author was picking out lines from
the longer text in any order that he pleased! But the reverse
must be the case. I see no other solution to the puzzle but that
those lines in the first part of AE must have remained alive and
precisely memorable in my father's mind (or perhaps he held all
of it in memory), and when he came later to write a much fuller
poem on Arthur's campaign they reappeared, even in altogether
different contexts. So the ravens that were croaking and the
eagles that were wheeling, and the wolves that were howling

on the wood's border, after the raids of the Saxon robbers and destroyers, reappear in lonely lands far removed from the coasts of Britain. And 'the wolves were howling on the wood's border' in the first line of the fourth canto of *The Fall of Arthur*.

But beyond the point reached above AE changes to become for fifty lines a very close forerunner of Canto I in the text LT, beginning:

> To Arthur spake he   evil tidings: (I.151–200)
> Too long my lord   from your land ye tarry!
> While war ye wage   on the wild people
> in the houseless East ………

with only very slight divergences here and there. Then, from 'and tarnished shields of truant knights / our numbers swell' (I.200–1) AE omits I.202–15, thus

> our numbers swell.   What need ye more?
> Is not Gawain true?   Hath not greater menace
> aforetime fled   that we faced together?   (I.216)

and continues to the end as in the final form, with 'anger' for 'vengeance' as the final word of the canto.

My father struck through with single pencil strokes the whole of the AE text, which ends here. In all the mass of draft papers for *The Fall of Arthur* there is no other element relating to Canto I save a single isolated page, very clearly written, beginning with the words 'thou wilt find their [*read*

thy] friends as foes meet thee' (I.194). It is obviously the only
suriving page of a text of Canto I that either immediately
preceded LT or was at one further remove from it. It scarcely
differs from the text in LT except for the lines following 'to
the Isle of Avalon, armies countless', that is I.205–210, whch
in this text read as follows:

> knights more noble   of renown fairer,
> men more mighty,   nor our match in prowess,
> wouldst thou ever assemble.   Here is earth's blossom
> that men shall remember   through the mists of time
> as a golden summer   ere the grey winter.

This is a convenient place to record several substantial corrections, made carefully in ink to the latest text of Canto I.

(I.9) Two lines following the words *booty seeking* were
struck out:

> raiding and ravaging.   His restless mood
> chafed as captive   in cage enchained.

(I.25) 'Fell thy hand is' was a correction of 'Fleet thy ships are'.

(I.43) After 'o'er many kingdoms' the line 'to misty Mirkwood's
margin dreary' was struck out; see pp.87, 209.

(I.56) After 'As in last sortie   from leaguered city' the following
lines were struck out:

when sudden the siege   is swept backward
and daring men   their doom almost
reverse by valour   vain and splendid
against hope and hazard   and a host of foes,
so Gawain led them.

(I.110–13) As the manuscript was written these lines read
before correction:

There evening came
with misty moon;   mournful breezes
in the wake of the winds   wailed in the branches,
where strands of storm ....

*

Canto II

I have shown earlier (see pp.173–4) that in my father's
original conception *The Fall of Arthur* was to begin with the
coming of the Frisian ship and Mordred's visit to Guinevere
in Camelot: the earliest texts give the opening canto the
number I, and describe the content in these words: 'How the
Frisian ship brought news and Mordred gathers his army to
stay the king's landing.'

The earliest manuscript of the canto, which I have called
IIa (p.173), extends as far as line II.109 in the final text. In
the first draft, which it seems was quickly replaced in this
respect, Mordred was actually to visit Guinevere before
anything was said of the news brought by the captain of

the wrecked vessel. Mordred looked from the window 'in his western tower' (II.20), as the 'sea far below sucked and laboured'; then follows at once:

> To Guenaver the golden,   with gleaming limbs
> that minds of men   with madness filled,
> his thought was turned,   thirst-tormented.
> He stepped on a stair   steep-winding down
> to her blissful bower ...

But this was rewritten (at once, as it appears):

> His thought was turned,   thirst-tormented,
> to Gwenaver the golden,   whose gleaming limbs
> the minds of men   with madness filled,
> so fair and fell,   frail and stony,
> true and faithless.   Towers might he conquer
> and thrones overthrow   and thirst slake not.
> In her blissful bower ...

The rewritten passage was now close to the form in LT (see II.25–32), and the 'stair steep-winding' (II.42) no longer goes down, but leads upward to the battlements of the castle.

I record in what follows further differences in the earliest text (*IIa*) of Canto II and the second text *IIb* (p.174) from LT, leaving out the many changes (often made for metrical reasons) that consist in the substitution of a single word

or changes in word-order. It may be noted that many of
the readings of *IIb* survived into LT and were rejected and
replaced after that text had been written. The reading of LT
is indicated by reference to the lines as printed in this book.

(II.47–65) Text *IIa* has here:

> Servants sought him,   soft-foot running,
> through hall and lodge   hunting swiftly.
> Before the queen's chamber,   closed and guarded,
> doubtful they halted   at doors of oak.
> Then Ivor his squire   the eager words
> let loudly ring: 'My lord!' he called,
> 'Tidings await thee –   time is passing!
> Come swiftly forth!   The sea spares us
> a shrift too short.'   He shook fiercely
> doors strong-timbered.   Drowsed and glowering
> Mordred answered,   and men trembled
> as he stood there stony   staring grimly:
> 'Mighty tidings,   that ye murder sleep
> ransacking with rabble   my royal castle!'
> Ivor him answered: 'Thine errand running
> the Frisian captain   on flying wings
> hath fled from France   but his fated ship
> is broken on the beach.   He is breathing still,
> but life is waning   and his lips wander.
> All else are dead.'

In *IIb* and in LT Ivor's reply to Mordred was retained from *IIa*; II.60–4 were an emendation in the latter.

(II.70–3) These lines were a pencilled addition in LT; *IIa* and *IIb* have here:

Cradoc the accursed   hath thy counsel bewrayed,
in Arthur's ears   all is rumoured ...

(II.80–4) *IIa* and *IIb* have here:

Whitesand with boats,   wherries and barges,
is crowded as with conclave   of clamorous gulls.
Shining on bulwarks ...

(II.90–1) *IIa* has here (*IIb* as in LT):

faithful to hatred   and faith scorning
his troth keeping   to traitor lord
died as his doom was.

(II.101–5) *IIa* has here, repeated in *IIb* with 'falsensss' for 'fickleness':

through the land of Logres   to lords and earls
whom he trusted that their tryst   they would truly
    hold
faithful in fickleness,   foes of Arthur,
lovers of Lancelot,   lightly purchased ...

This passage survived into the LT manuscript, where the text that replaced it was written in the margin.

(II.108–9)   Both *IIa* and *IIb* have here, where *IIa* ends:

> of Almain and Angel   and isles of the North,
> cormorants of the coast   and the cold marshes.

In all the following entries the text given is that of *IIb* (before any emendation) with the corresponding LT line reference in the margin.

(II.110–20)   He came to Camelot   the queen seeking;
> greedily he gazed on her   with glittering eyes;
> her grey eyes gaily   his glance challenged,
> proud and pitiless,   yet pale her cheek;

In LT my father repeated this passage, but struck it out and replaced it on a separate page with the longer text beginning 'Fiercely heard she his feet hasten' at line 111. At line 119 the word *chill* was a replacement, with a query, of *still*.

(II.128–33)   to no noise of knighthood.   Nights are weary.
> Yet less than beloved   or lower than queen
> life here below   shalt thou lead never.
> A king courts thee ...

A pencilled change replaced this in *IIb*:

THE FALL OF ARTHUR

to no noise of knighthood. Yet never shalt thou
live unbeloved, nor less than queen,
though chances change – if thou choose aright.´

The final text of LT was written in the margin of the manuscript.

(II.144–7)   For the text of *IIb* here see p.175.

(II.157–65)   my thirst slaking;
             for life is loathsome   by longing haunted;
             I will be king after   and crowned with gold.'
             Then Guinever the proud,   aghast in mind,
             between fear and loathing,   who in former day
             wielding beauty   was wont rather
             to be sought than seized,   dissembling spake:
             'Eagerly my lord   do ye urge your suit!
             Delay allow me ...

(II.176–7)   These lines are absent in *IIb*.

(II.213)   and time's new tide turn to her purpose.

                         *

Cantos IV and V

In Canto IV the textual history is readily followed. The first
manuscript, which would be constantly unintelligible without
the later texts as a guide, is less a text of the poem than a record
of my father 'thinking with his pen'. It may be that he was to

some extent giving written form to verse that he had already prepared and memorised, but it is clear that he was also composing *ab initio,* experimenting as he went, often setting down several variants of an alliterative phase.

This manuscript was already remarkably close to the text of the latest version. Following it is a hastily written but legible text, somewhat emended in the usual fashion, leading to the text (LT) as printed. One passage of the canto in LT was rejected and another, longer version (IV.137–154) written, equally carefully in ink, on a separate sheet: the rejected text reads as follows:

At Arthur's side   eager hastened
a mighty ship   in the morn gleaming
high, white-timbered,   with hull gilded;
on its sail was sewn   a sun rising,
on its broidered banner   in the breeze floated
a griffon glowing   as with golden fire.
Thus Gawain came   his king guarding
to the van hasting.   Now to view came all:
a hundred ships   with hulls shining,
and shrouds swelling   and shields swinging.
Ten thousand told   targes hung there ...

The few pencilled alterations to the text may be mentioned:
line 24 'like drops of glass   dripped and glistened' replaced
'like tears of glass   gleamed and tinkled';
lines 98–9 were a marginal addition;
lines 209–10 'as stalks falling / before reapers ruthless, as

roke flying' replaced 'as starlings fleeing / from reapers ruthless, as roke melting'.

Lastly, the title of the canto as I have given it, 'How
Arthur returned at morn and by Sir Gawain's hand won the
passage of the sea', was a replacement of the original title
written in ink 'Of the setting of the sun at Romeril' – which
became the title of Canto V.

Of the the fifth canto no draft material in verse survives.

*

APPENDIX

APPENDIX:
OLD ENGLISH VERSE

The importance of the use of Old English 'alliterative verse' in my father's sole 'Arthurian' poem seems to call for some indication, within the pages of this book, of its essential nature, preferably in his own words. His account of the ancient verse-form is indeed well known, appearing in his 'Prefatory Remarks' to the new edition (1940) by C.L. Wrenn of the translation of *Beowulf* by J.R. Clark Hall; these 'Prefatory Remarks' have been reprinted in *J.R.R. Tolkien: The Monsters and the Critics and Other Essays*, 1983. I have also cited a portion of it in *The Legend of Sigurd and Gudrún*, 2009.

On 14 January 1938 there was broadcast by the BBC a brief recorded talk by my father entitled 'Anglo-Saxon Verse'. On this he expended much thought and labour, as is attested by a great deal of preliminary drafting, but here all that need be said is that there is also a later and much longer lecture on the subject, addressed to some audience actually present, clearly related to the broadcast talk but very distinct. For the present book I think it may be interesting to print some passages extracted, with minor editing, from this lecture, very different in scope and manner though belonging to the same period as the *Prefatory Remarks.*

For exemplification my father took the concluding lines of the Old English poem *The Battle of Brunanburh*, and gave an alliterative translation. The text of the lecture was subsequently much emended and many passages were marked for omission, perhaps for considerations of time. The date that appears in the first line, '1006 this autumn', i.e. 1943 as the year of composition, was changed first to '1008' and then to '1011 last autumn'; this presumably means that it was repeated in other places in those years.

> Ne wearð wæl máre
> on þýs églande   æfre gýta
> folces gefylled   beforan þyssum
> sweordes wecgum,   þæs þe ús secgað béc,
> ealde úþwitan,   syððan éastan hider
> Engle and Seaxe   úp becómon
> ofer brád brimu,   Brytene sóhton,
> wlance wígsmiþas   Wéalas ofercómon,
> eorlas árhwate   eard begéaton.

> No greater host
> of folk hath fallen   before this day
> in this island ever   by the edge of swords
> in battle slaughtered,   as books tell us
> and ancient authors,   since from the east hither
> Saxon and English   from the sea landed,
> over the broad billows   Britain assailing,

the Welsh smiting   on war's anvil,
glory seeking   great men of old,
in this land winning   a lasting home.

So sang a court poet 1000 years ago – 1006 this autumn to be precise: commemorating the great Battle of Brunanburh, AD 937. So great was it that it was long remembered as *magnum bellum*. The victor was Æthelstan, Ælfred's grandson, one of the greatest monarchs of the day. His enemies were an alliance of Norse, Scots, and Welsh kings and chieftains. These lines are the ending of a short poem (73 lines long) that is embedded in the so-called 'Anglo-Saxon Chronicle'. So it comes from the tenth century; the century of the great Æthelwulfing kings (descendants, that is, of Æthelwulf and Ælfred his son), when the English revived after the havoc of the ninth century. It is from the tenth century that we derive most of the documents, of prose and of verse, that have survived the later wrecks of time. The older world, before the Norse invasions, had passed away in ruin. All that has come down to us from that earlier time, the first flowering time of English verse, is preserved in tenth-century copies – all but a very few scraps.

It is in the records of the fifth century that the word 'Anglo-Saxon' first appears. Indeed it was King Æthelstan who, among other high titles such as *Bretwalda* and *Caesar*, first styled himself *Ongulsaxna cyning*, that is, 'King of Angel-Saxons'. But he did *not* speak 'Anglo-Saxon', for there never was such a language. The king's language was then, as now, *Englisc:* English. If you have ever heard that Chaucer was the 'father of English poetry', forget it. English poetry has no recorded father, even as a written art, and the beginning lies beyond our view, in the mists of northern antiquity.

To speak of Anglo-Saxon language is thus wrong and misleading. You can speak of an 'Anglo-Saxon period' in history, before 1066. But it is not a very useful label. There was no such thing as a single uniform 'Anglo-Saxon' period. The *fifth century*, and the coming of the English to Britain, to which the poet of *Brunanburh* referred in the *tenth century*, was as remote from him in time, and as different from his days in kind, as the Wars of the Roses are from us.

But there it is: 'the Anglo-Saxon period' covers six centuries. During that long age a great vernacular literature (to speak only of that) – I mean a 'literature' in the full sense, books written by cultivated and learned men – had arisen, and been ruined, and again to some extent revived. What is left today is only a tattered fragment of a very great wealth. But as far as can be seen from what is preserved, there is one feature common to all the verse of the period, older and later. That is the ancient English metre and technique of verse. It is quite unlike modern metres and methods, both in its rules and in its aims. It is often called 'alliterative' verse – and I will say a word on that in a moment. The 'alliterative' measures were used throughout the Anglo-Saxon period for *poetry in English*; and for English poetry only 'alliterative' verse was used. It did not, however, stop at 1066! It went on being used for at least four hundred years longer in the North and West. In the kind of verse meant for books (and so for educated people, clerical or lay) this 'alliterative' technique was elaborate and highly polished. It was used because it was admired and appreciated by cultivated men, and not simply because the poor 'Saxons' knew nothing else, for in point of fact they did. The English of those days were interested in verse and often quite accomplished metrists, and could when writing in Latin use many classical metres or compose in what we call 'rhyme'.

Now this 'alliterative' metre has great virtues in itself. I mean that it is quite worthy of study by poets today as a technique. But it is also interesting as being a native art independent of classical models (I mean, as a metre: I am not talking about matter: the ancient English poets of those days often used alliterative verse for matter that they had got out of Greek and Latin books). It was already old in Alfred's day. Indeed it descends from days before the English came to Britain, and is almost identical with the metre used for the oldest Norse (Norwegian and Icelandic) poems. A great body of oral verse dealing with ancient days in the northern lands was known to minstrels in England, though little has survived beyond one long verse catalogue [*Widsith*] of the subjects of heroic and legendary song: a list of now forgotten or almost forgotten kings and heroes.

It would take an hour or two to explain properly the Old English metre and show how it works, and what kind of things it can do and what it cannot. In essence it is made by taking the half-dozen commonest and most compact phrase-patterns of the ordinary language that have two main elements or stresses – for example (lines from the translation of the passage from *The Battle of Brunanburh*):

	A	*glóry séeking*
	B	*by the édge of swórds*
	C	*from the séa lánded*
	E	*gréat men of óld*
[added later:	D	*brígt árchàngels*]

Two of these, usually different, are balanced against one another to make a full line. They are linked or cemented together by what is usually but wrongly called 'alliteration'. It is not 'alliteration' because it does not depend on letters or spelling, but on sounds: it is in fact a kind of brief rhyme: head-rhyme.

The chief syllable – loudest (most stressed), highest in tone, and most significant – in each half must begin with the same consonant, or agree in beginning with a vowel (i.e. no consonant).

So	in **b**attle **s**laughtered as **b**ooks tell us
or	**gl**ory **s**eeking **gr**eat men of old
or	**a**ncient **au**thors since from the **ea**st hither

In the last example there are *two* head-rhymes or 'staves' in the first half-line. That is often the case, but not compulsory. In the second half *two* are not allowed. The *first* important syllable, and that only, must 'bear the stave' or rhyme. This has important consequences. It means that you must always so arrange your phrases that the most important word comes first in the second half-line. There is thus always a drop in force, loudness, and significance at the end of an Old English line, and then the spring is wound up again at the beginning.

Very frequently the beginning of a new line repeats in more vigorous form, or produces some variation on, the end of the preceding line:

as books tell us // ancient authors
from the sea landed // over the broad billows

So all Old English verse is rich in parallelisms and verbal variations.

But there is of course a good deal more in Old English verse beside the mere sound patterns. There was the vocabulary and diction. It was 'poetical'. Already in the first written survivals of English verse we find a rich vocabulary of poetry-words – and then as now these words were to a large extent *archaisms*, old words and forms that had fallen out of daily use in some senses, or altogether, but had been preserved by poetic tradition.

Kennings. Poetic 'riddling' expressions, sometimes called *kennings* (an Icelandic word meaning 'descriptions'), are a marked feature of Old English verse diction, especially in more elaborate poems, and are one of its chief poetic weapons. Thus a poet may say *bán-hús* 'bone-house' and mean 'body'; but mean you also (though with almost lighting swiftness) to think of a house being built with its wooden frame and beams and between them the clay packed and shaped in the old style, and then see the parallelism between that and skeleton and flesh. He may say *beado-léoma* 'flame of battle' and mean 'sword' – a bright blade drawn in the sun with a sudden flash; and similarly *merehengest* 'sea-stallion' for 'ship'; *ganotes bæð* 'the gannet's bathing-place' for 'sea'. The Old English poet liked pictures, but valued them the more sudden, hard and compact they were. He did not unroll similes. You had to be attentive and quick-witted to catch all that he meant and saw.

In the Chronicle poem of the Battle of Brunanburh the poet speaks of *wlance wigsmiþas* overthrowing the Welsh – literally 'splendid war-smiths'. You can say if you like that 'war-smith' is 'just a kenning in verse' for 'warrior': so it is in mere logic and syntax. But it was coined and used to mean 'warrior' and at the same time to give a sound-picture and an eye-picture of battle. We miss it, because none of us have seen or heard a battle of steel or iron weapons hand-wielded, and few now have seen an old-fashioned smith hammering iron on an anvil. The clang of such a battle could be heard a long way off: like a lot of men hammering on metal bars and hacking at iron-cooped barrels, or – very much like, for those who have heard it (as everyone had in those days), a smith beating out a plough-share, or forging chain-links: not one smith, though, but hundreds all in competition. And seen closer too, the rise and fall of swords and axes would remind men of smiths swinging hammers.

I have no more time to give to Old English verse methods. But you will see that it has some interest. And the attempt to translate it is not a bad exercise for training in the full appreciation of words – a thing already all people are perilously slack in nowadays: though it is really impossible. Our language now has becone quick-moving (in syllables), and may be very supple and nimble, but is rather thin in sound and in sense too often diffuse and vague. The language of our forefathers, especially in verse, was slow, not very nimble, but very sonorous, and was intensely packed and concentrated – or could be in a good poet.

Appended to this lecture are four passages from my father's own 'alliterative' works. The first is *Winter Comes to Nargothrond* in the third version, almost exactly as in *The Lays of Beleriand* (1985), p.129. The second is a passage from the alliterative *Lay of the Children of Húrin, ibid.*, lines 1554–70, with many minor differences (a much developed version is given in *The Lays of Beleriand*, pp.129–30).

Most notably, the third and fourth extracts are taken from *The Fall of Arthur*. The first of these, as written in ink, consists of III.1–10 (*In the south from sleep ...*) differing only in points of punctuation; later my father pencilled in the next four lines, to *Dark slowly fell* (which he marked wth 'D'), and wrote against the extract *Descriptive Style*.

The second extract from *The Fall of Arthur* runs from I.183 to 211 and agrees exactly with the text given in this book except that line I.200 *and tarnished shields   of truant lieges* is omitted, and there is a different reading at line 207, *upon mortal earth* for *under moon and sun*. A notable feature of this text is that against each line my father wrote the relevant letters referring to the patterns of strong and weak elements ('lifts' and 'dips') in each half-line (see pp.227–8 above).

Arthur speaks:

B	C	Now for Lancelot I long sorely
B	B	and we miss now most the mighty swords
C	A	of Ban's kindred. Best meseemeth
E	A	swift word to send, service craving
B	C	to their lord of old. To this leagued treason
B	A	we must power oppose, proud returning
B	A	with matchless might Mordred to humble.
A	A	Gawain answered grave and slowly:
A	C	Best meseemeth that Ban's kindred
+A	C	abide in Benwick and this black treason
A	B	favour nor further. Yet I fear the worse:
B	C	thou wilt find thy friends as foes meet thee.
B	C	If Lancelot hath loyal purpose
+A	B	let him prove repentance, his pride foregoing,
C	C	uncalled coming when his king needeth.
+A	A	But fainer with fewer faithful-hearted
C	B	would I dare danger, than with doubtful swords
B	C	our muster swell. Why more need we?
B	B	Though thou legions levy through the lands
		of Earth,
A	C	fay or mortal, from the Forest's margin
+A	A	to the Isle of Avalon, armies countless,
A	A	never and nowhere knights more puissant,
A	C	nobler chivalry of renown fairer,
A	B	mightier manhood upon mortal earth
B	C	shall be gathered again till graves open.

+A B Here free, unfaded,   is the flower of time
+A B that men shall remember   through the mist
       of years
    B C as a golden summer   in the grey winter.

It will be seen that there are no D half-lines and only one E in this extract. The sign +A is here used to indicate a prefixed dip or 'anacrusis' brfore the first lift in A half-lines. In lines 202 *Though thou legions levy* and 211 *as a golden summer*, both marked B, the words *levy* and *summer* constitute 'broken lifts', where instead of a long stressed syllable there is a short stressed followed by a weak syllable.

This extract has a designation of the style of the passage, which is scarcely legible, but could be interpreted as 'Dramatic and rhetorical'.

*